FAR OUT
FAIRY TALES

STONE ARCH BOOKS
a capstone imprint

INTRODUCING...

HANK MILLER

GUS

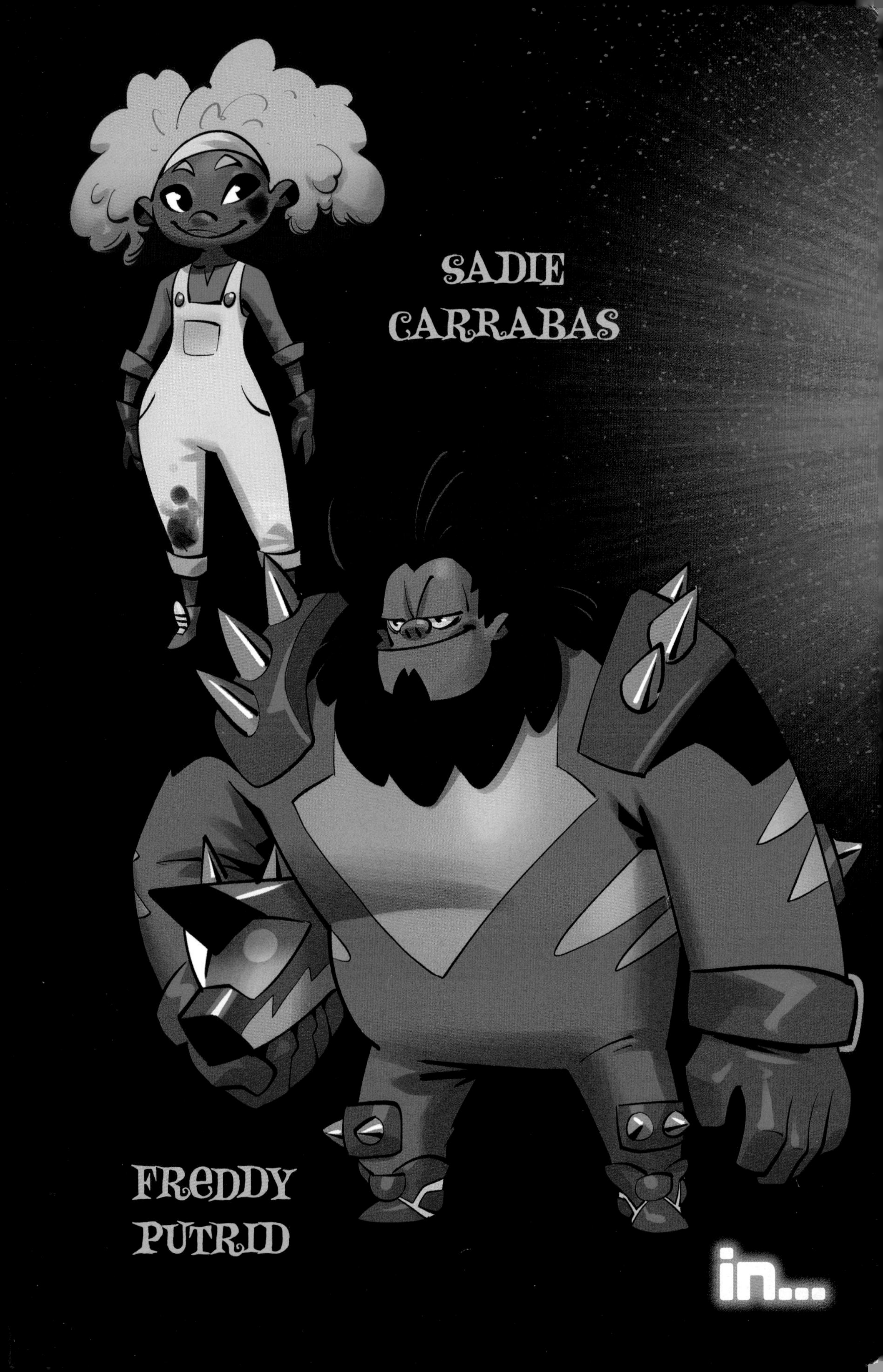
SADIE
CARRABAS
FREDDY
PUTRID
in...

Far Out Fairy Tales are published by
Stone Arch Books, an imprint of
Capstone.
1710 Roe Crest Drive
North Mankato, Minnesota 56003
www.capstonepub.com

Images on p. 32 from *Puss in Boots: A
Retelling of the Grimm's Fairy Tale*,
© 2011 Capstone Library of Congress

Library of Congress Cataloging-in-
Publication data is available on the
Library of Congress website.
ISBN 9781663910677 (hardcover)
ISBN 9781663921314 (paperback)
ISBN 9781663910646 (eBook pdf)

Summary: Mr. Alestair Miller, the
owner of Miller and Sons Auto
Emporium, has died. His oldest son
inherited his father's auto shop. The
middle son received his collection of
antique automobiles. And his youngest
son, Hank, was given his father's old
motocross bike and gear and his
pet cat, Gus. While Hank is initially
disappointed, he eventually learns that
his inheritance is actually the best of
all three brothers'.

Designed by Hilary Wacholz
Edited by Mandy Robbins
Lettered by Jaymes Reed

FAR OUT FAIRY TALES

PUSS in MAGICAL MOTOCROSS BOOTS

A GRAPHIC NOVEL

BY BRANDON TERRELL

ILLUSTRATED BY OMAR LOZANO

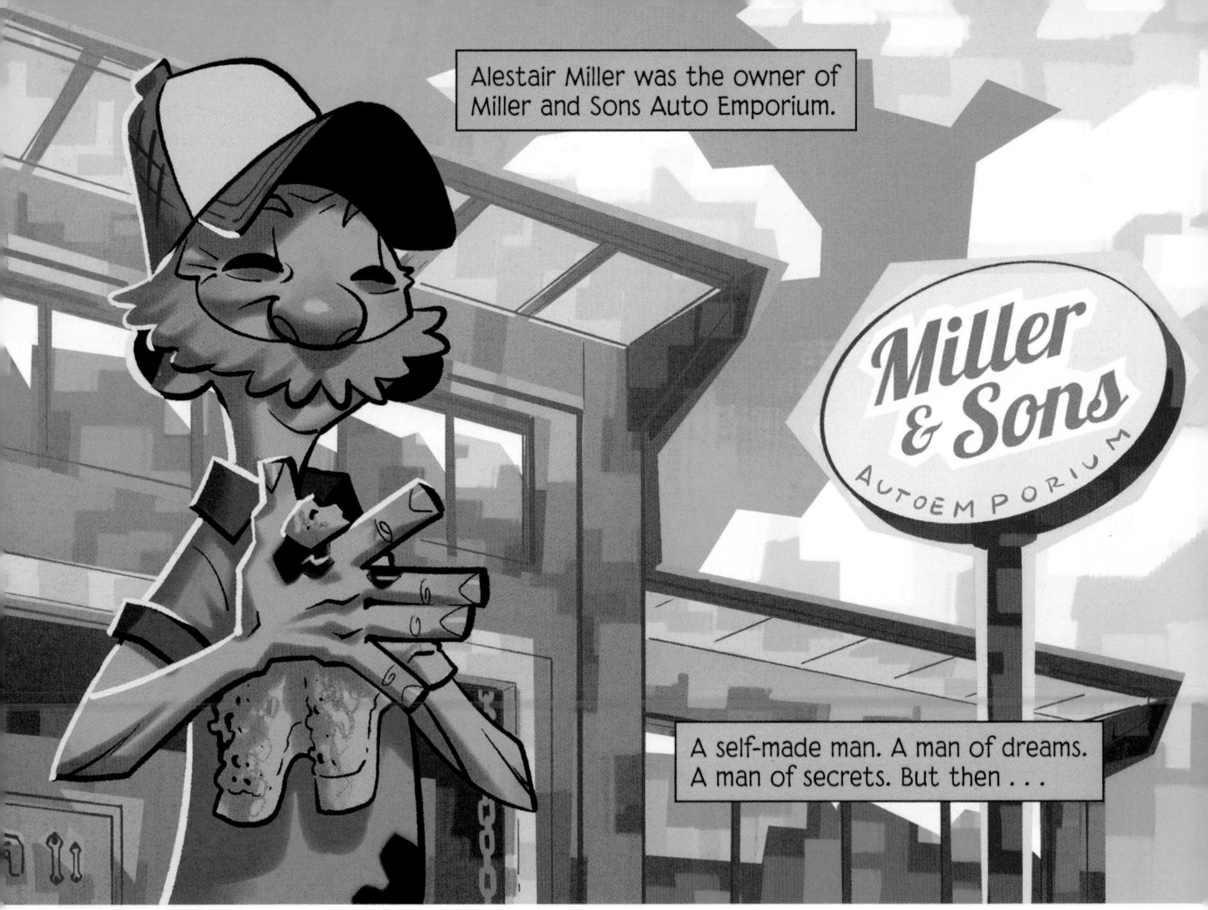
Alestair Miller was the owner of Miller and Sons Auto Emporium.
Miller & Sons
AUTOEMPORIUM
A self-made man. A man of dreams. A man of secrets. But then . . .

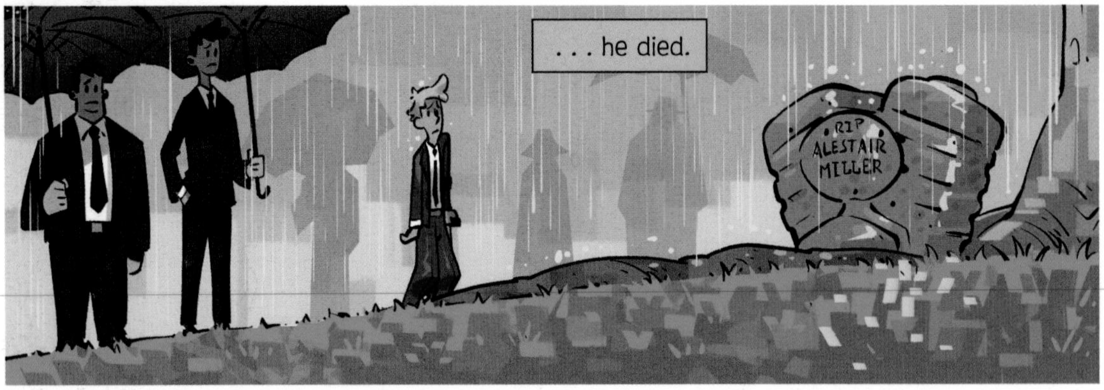
. . . he died.
RIP ALESTAIR MILLER

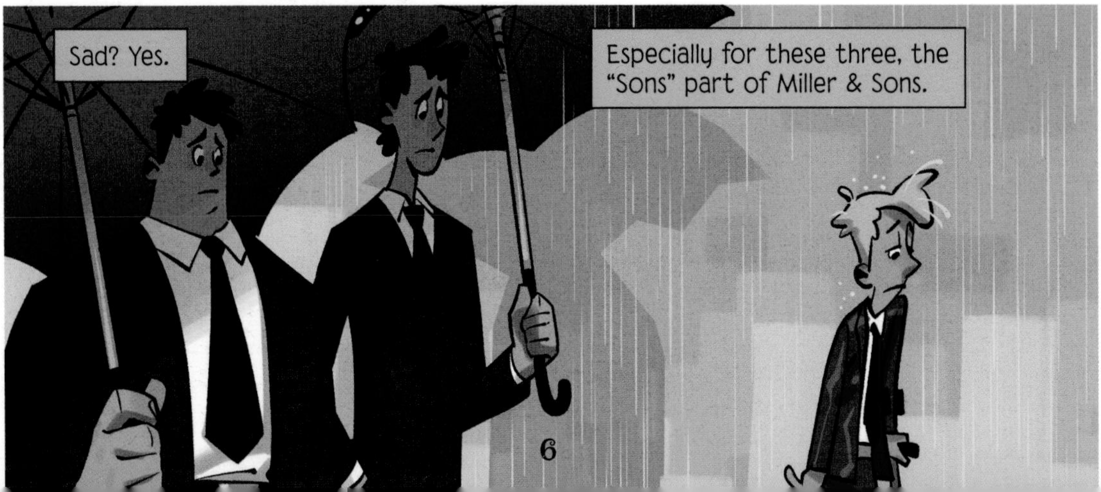
Sad? Yes.
Especially for these three, the "Sons" part of Miller & Sons.

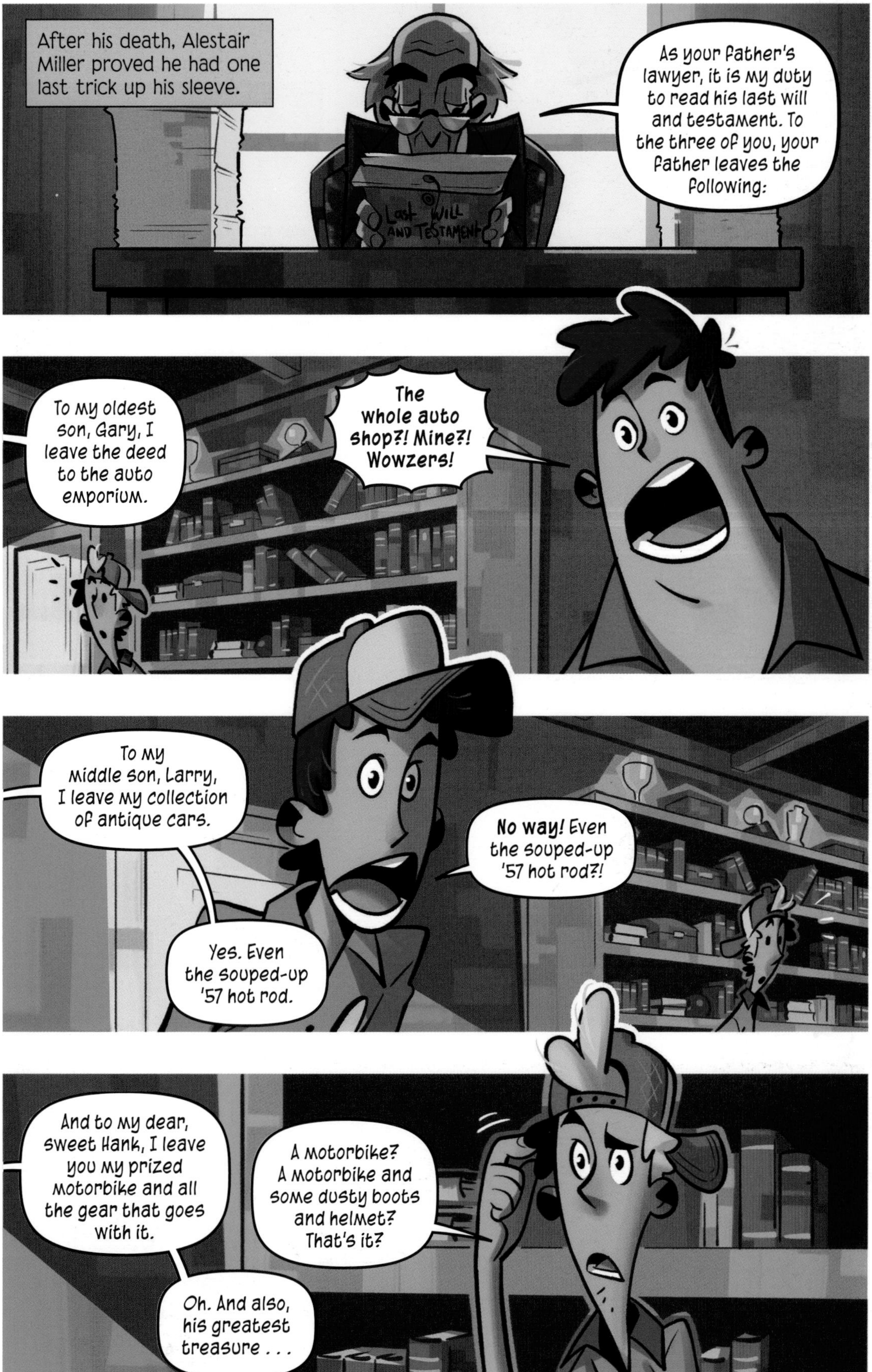
After his death, Alestair Miller proved he had one last trick up his sleeve.
LAST WILL AND TESTAMENT
As your father's lawyer, it is my duty to read his last will and testament. To the three of you, your father leaves the following:
To my oldest son, Gary, I leave the deed to the auto emporium.
The whole auto shop?! Mine?! Wowzers!
To my middle son, Larry, I leave my collection of antique cars.
No way! Even the souped-up '57 hot rod?!
Yes. Even the souped-up '57 hot rod.
And to my dear, sweet Hank, I leave you my prized motorbike and all the gear that goes with it.
A motorbike? A motorbike and some dusty boots and helmet? That's it?
Oh. And also, his greatest treasure . . .

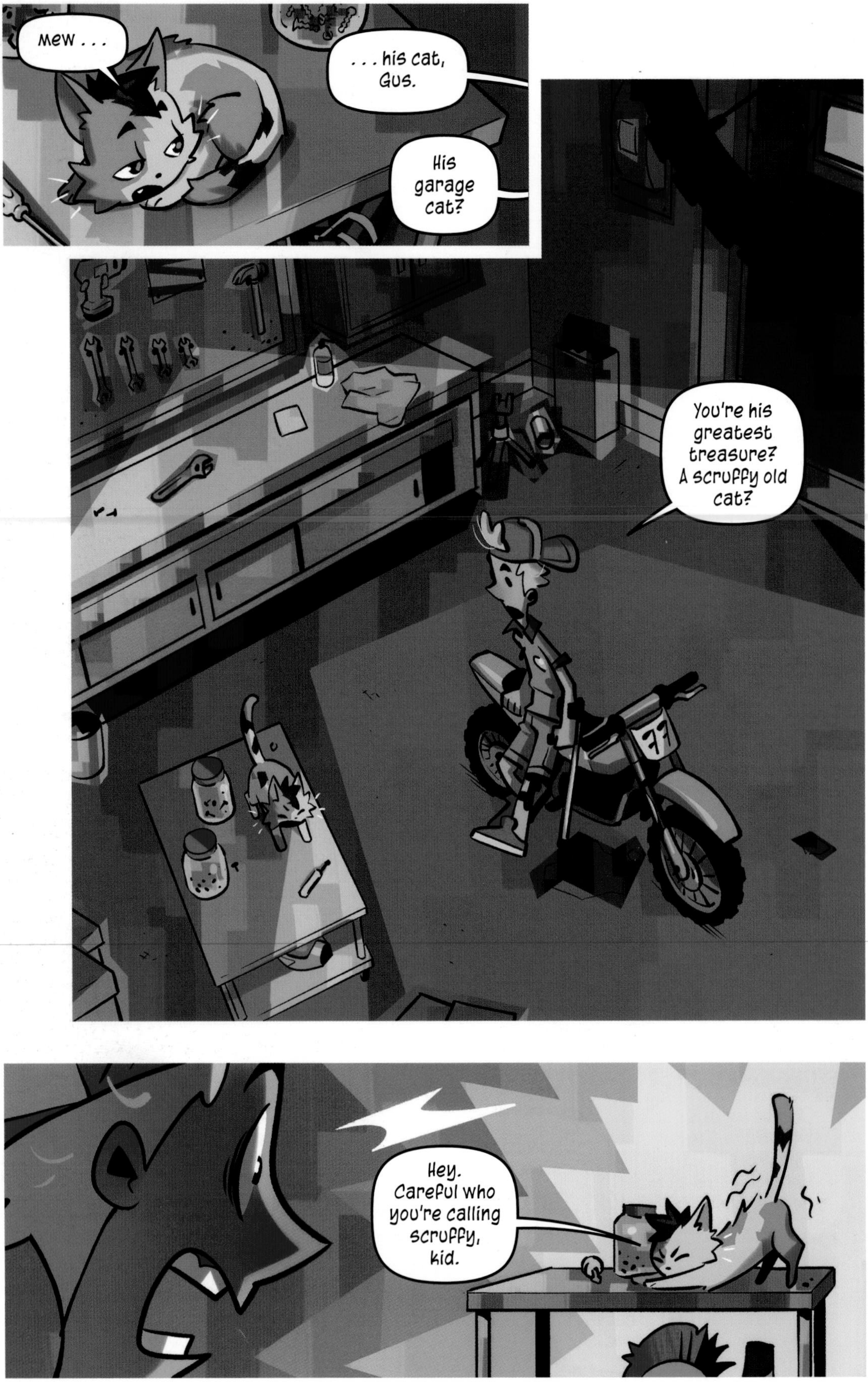
Mew . . .
. . . his cat, Gus.
His garage cat?
You're his greatest treasure? A scruffy old cat?
Hey. Careful who you're calling scruffy, kid.

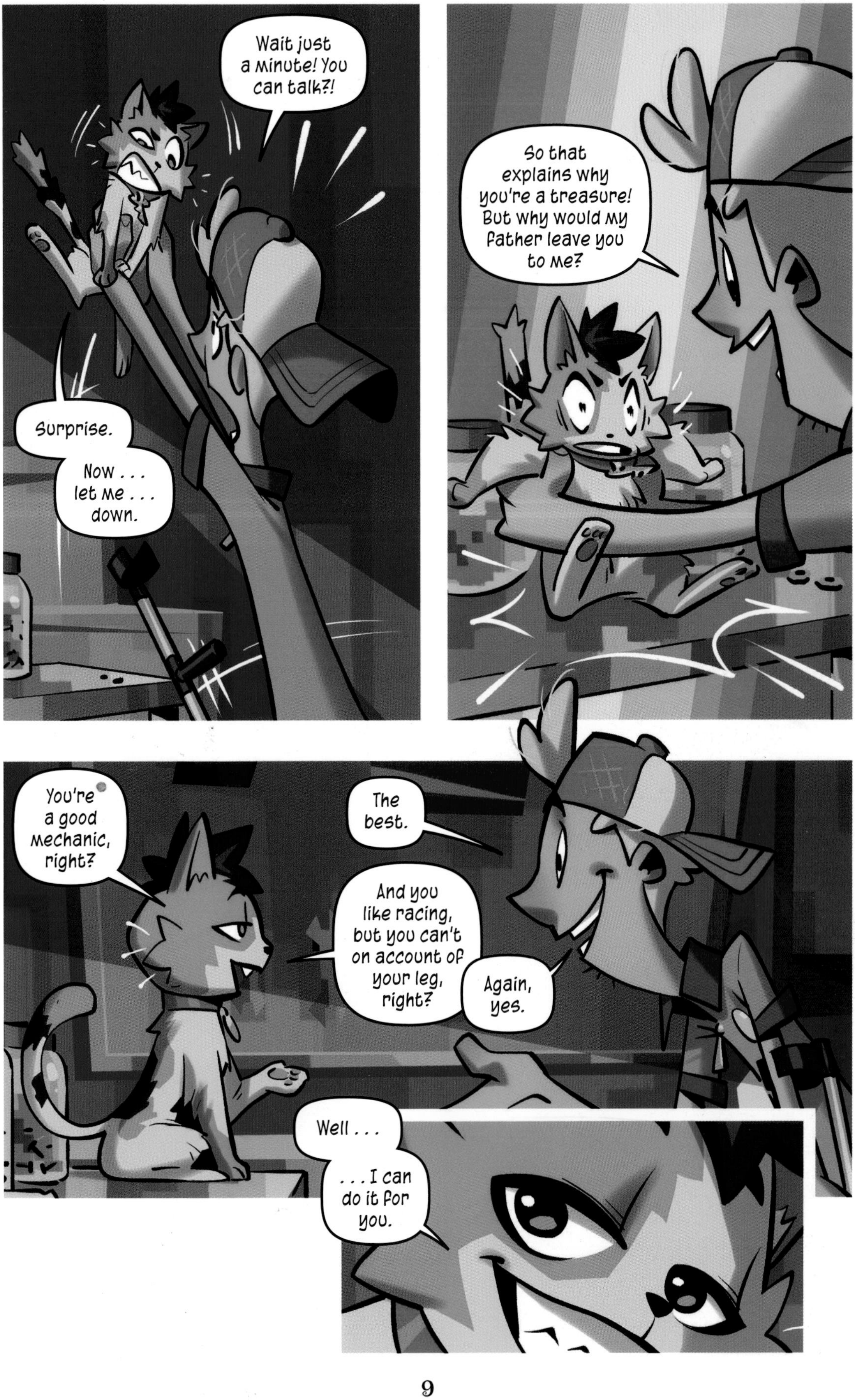
Wait just a minute! You can talk?!
Surprise.
Now . . . let me . . . down.
So that explains why you're a treasure! But why would my father leave you to me?
You're a good mechanic, right?
The best.
And you like racing, but you can't on account of your leg, right?
Again, yes.
Well . . .
. . . I can do it for you.

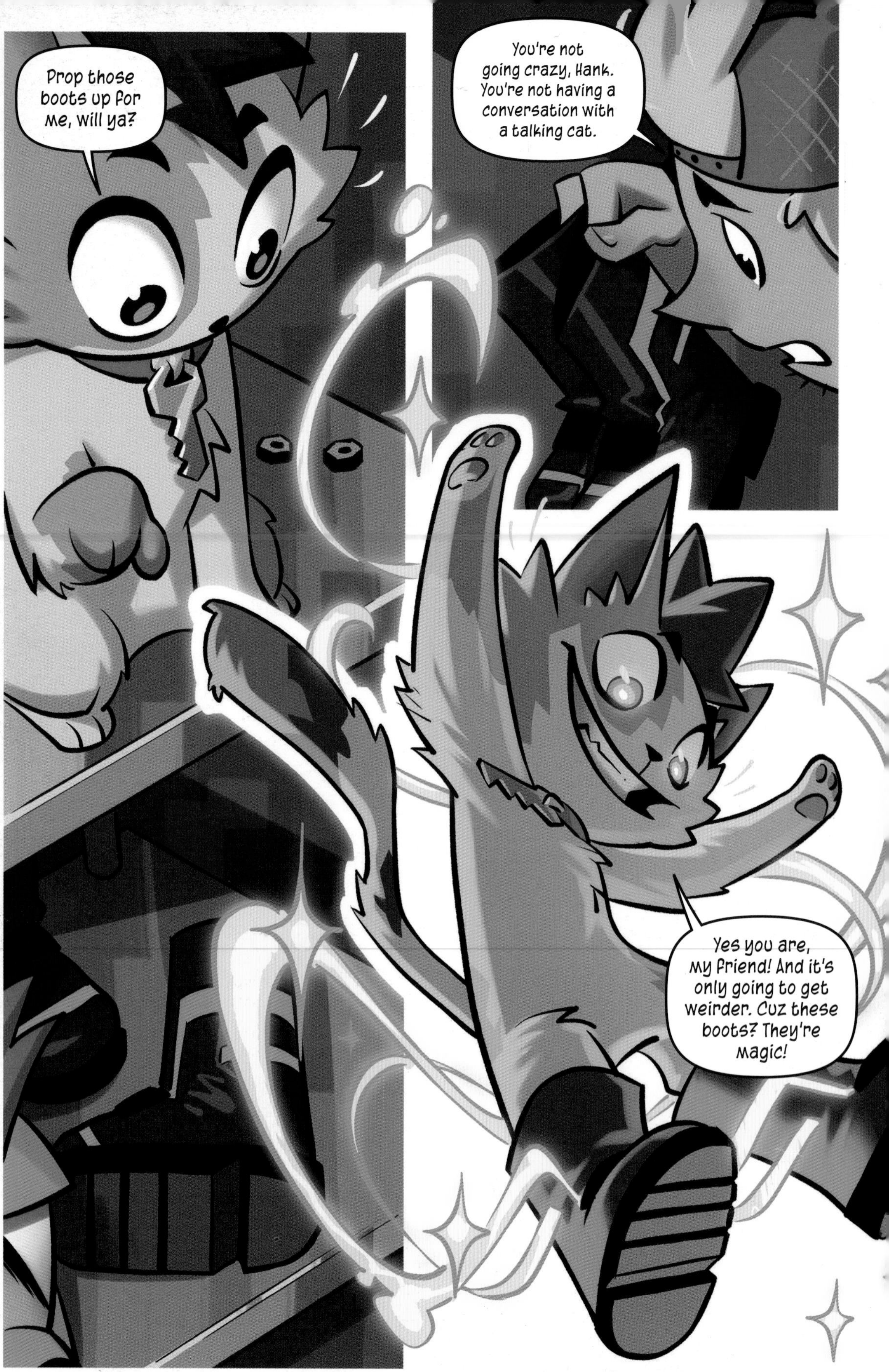
Prop those boots up for me, will ya?
You're not going crazy, Hank. You're not having a conversation with a talking cat.
Yes you are, my friend! And it's only going to get weirder. Cuz these boots? They're magic!

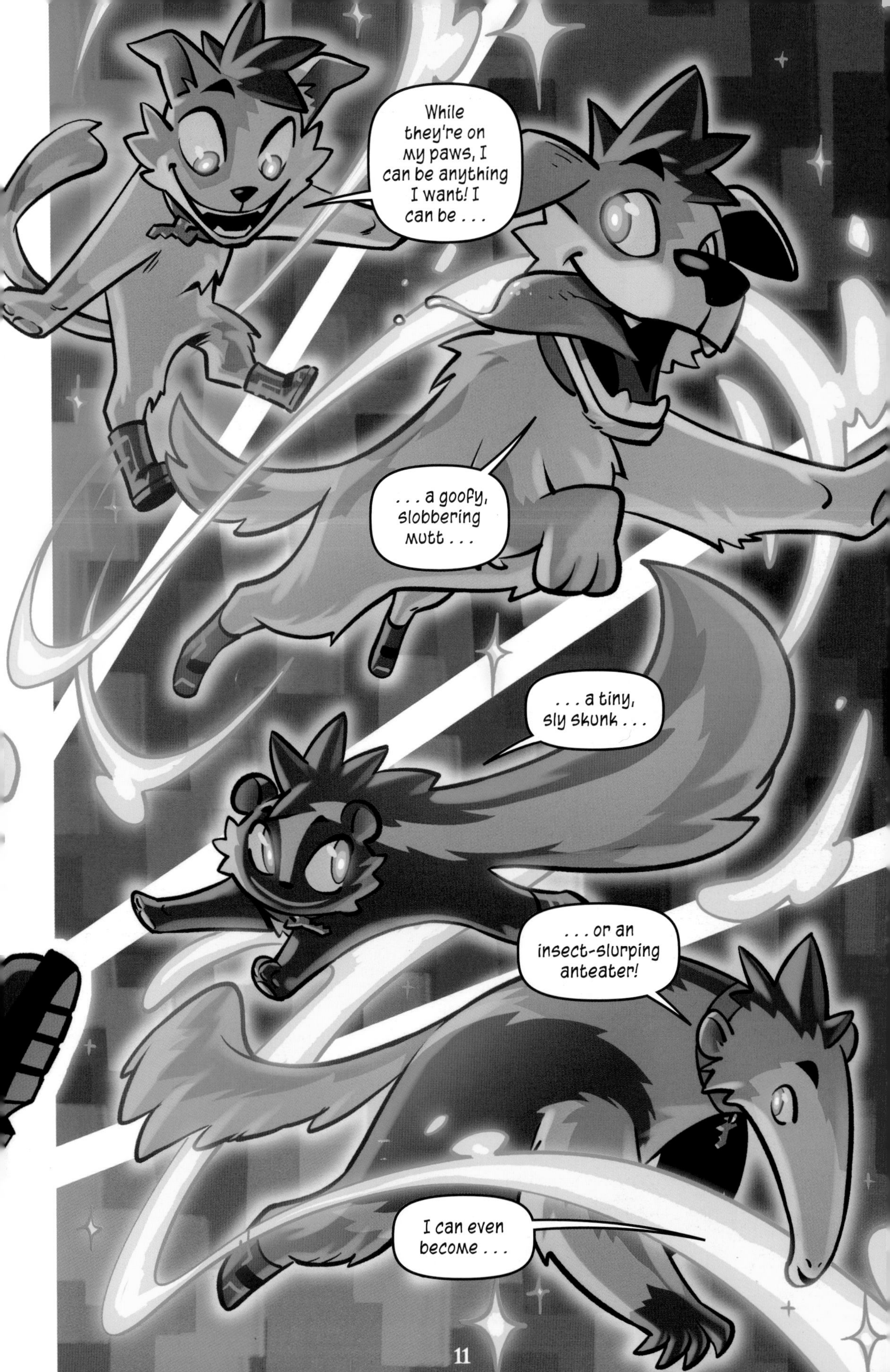

While they're on my paws, I can be anything I want! I can be . . .
. . . a goofy, slobbering mutt . . .
. . . a tiny, sly skunk . . .
. . . or an insect-slurping anteater!
I can even become . . .

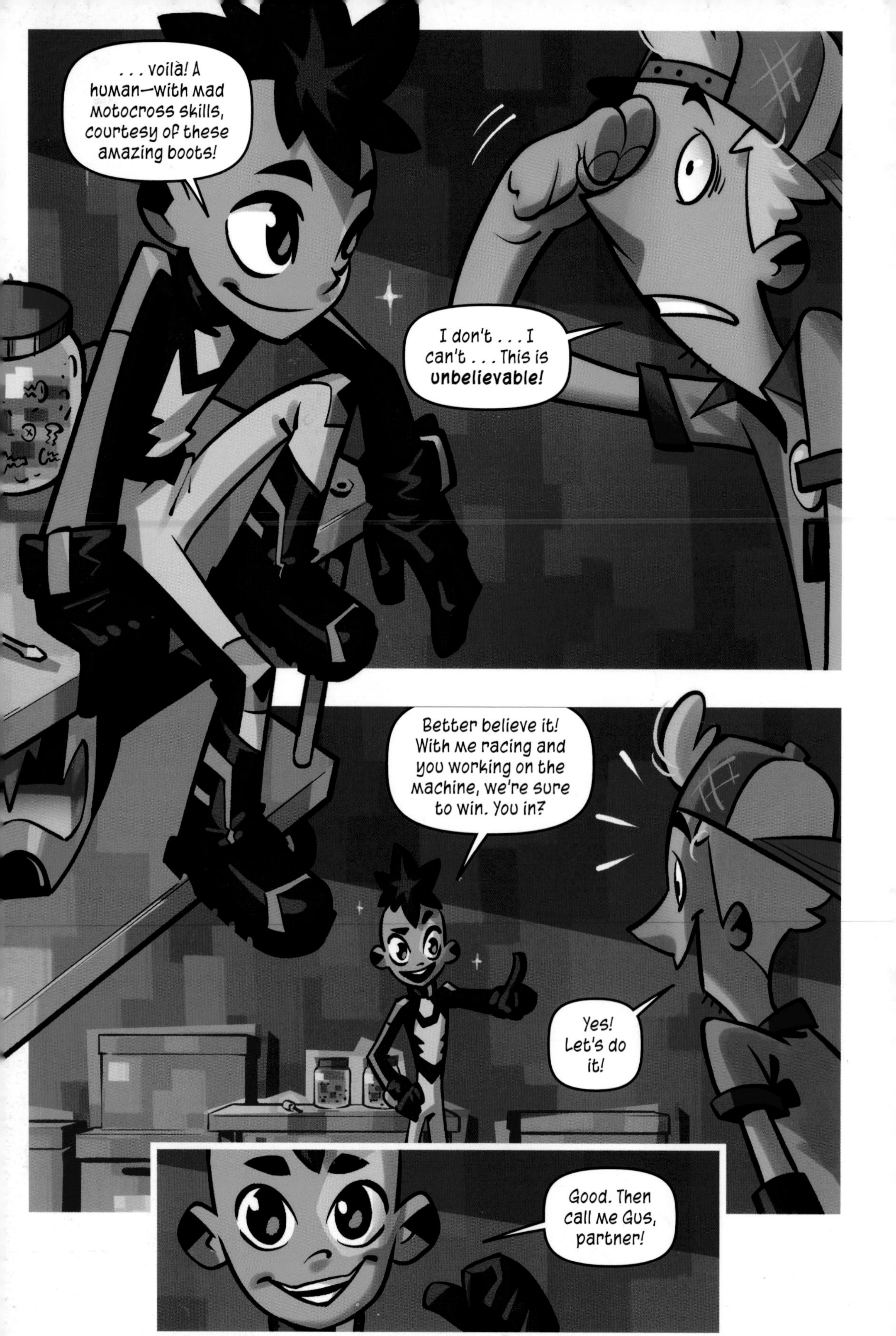

. . . voilà! A human—with mad motocross skills, courtesy of these amazing boots!
I don't . . . I can't . . . This is **unbelievable!**
Better believe it! With me racing and you working on the machine, we're sure to win. You in?
Yes! Let's do it!
Good. Then call me Gus, partner!

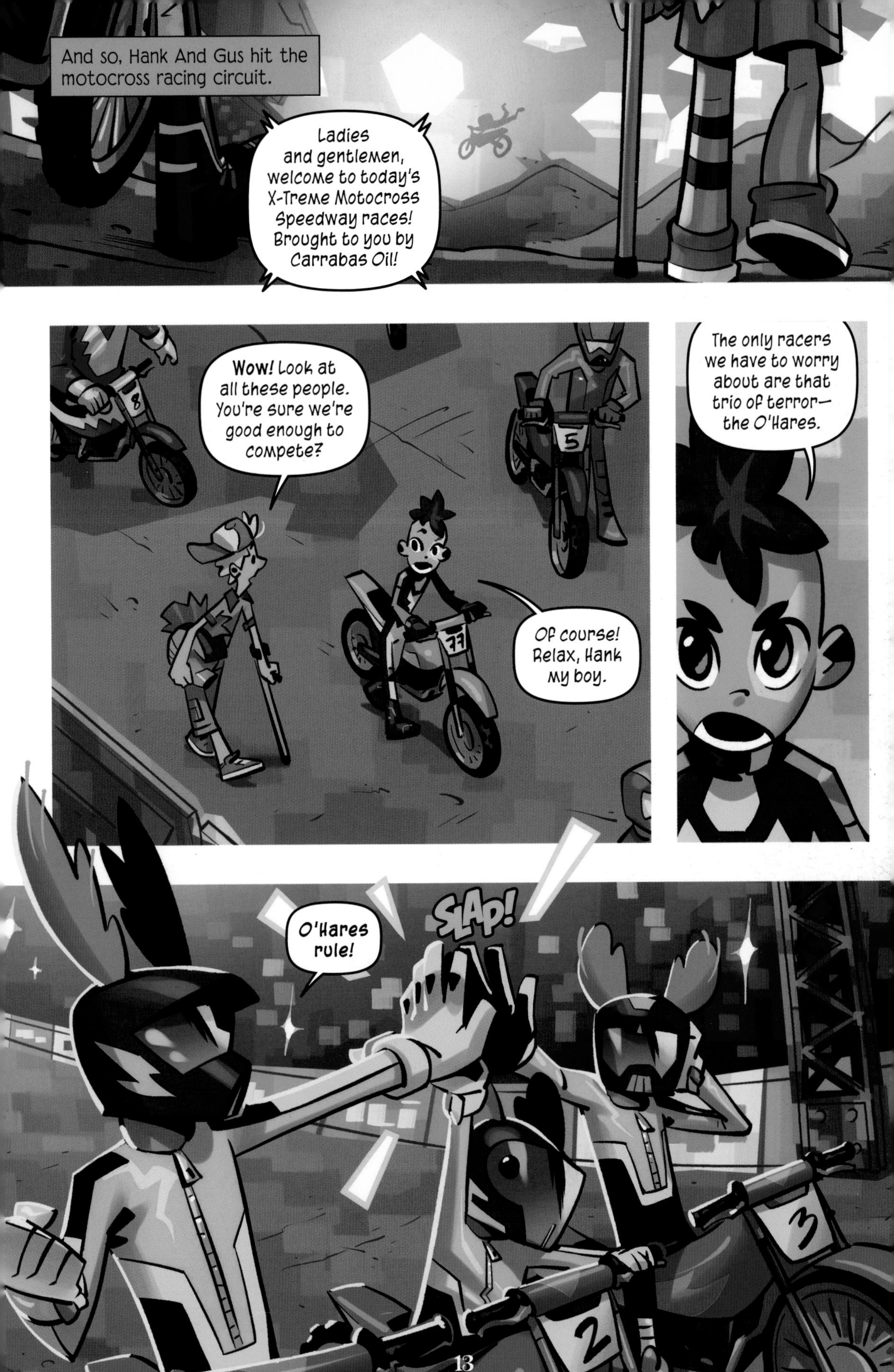

And so, Hank And Gus hit the motocross racing circuit.
Ladies and gentlemen, welcome to today's X-Treme Motocross Speedway races! Brought to you by Carrabas Oil!
Wow! Look at all these people. You're sure we're good enough to compete?
Of course! Relax, Hank my boy.
The only racers we have to worry about are that trio of terror— the O'Hares.
O'Hares rule!
SLAP!

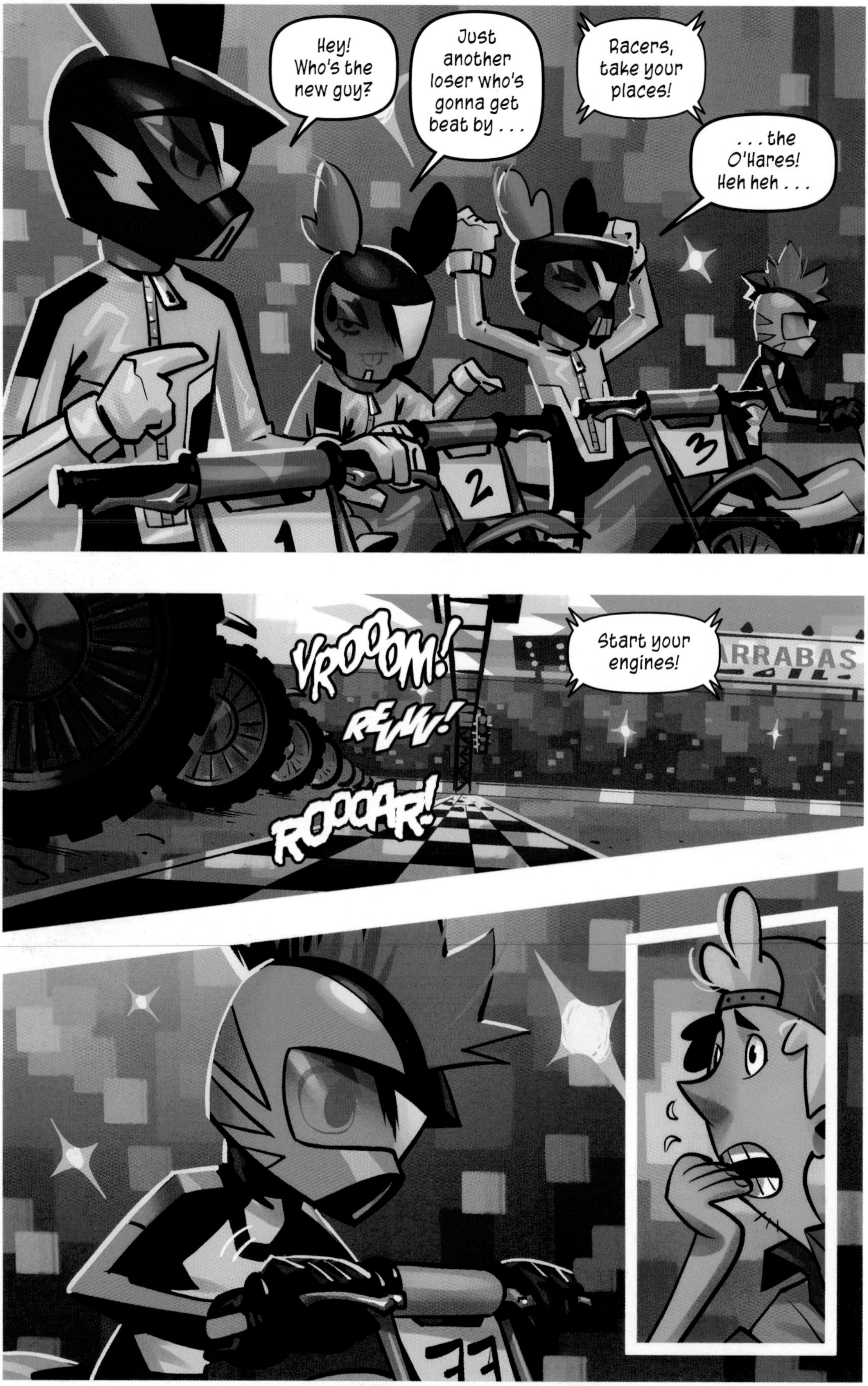
Hey! Who's the new guy?
Just another loser who's gonna get beat by . . .
Racers, take your places!
. . . the O'Hares! Heh heh . . .
VROOOOM!
REVVV!
ROOOAR!
Start your engines!

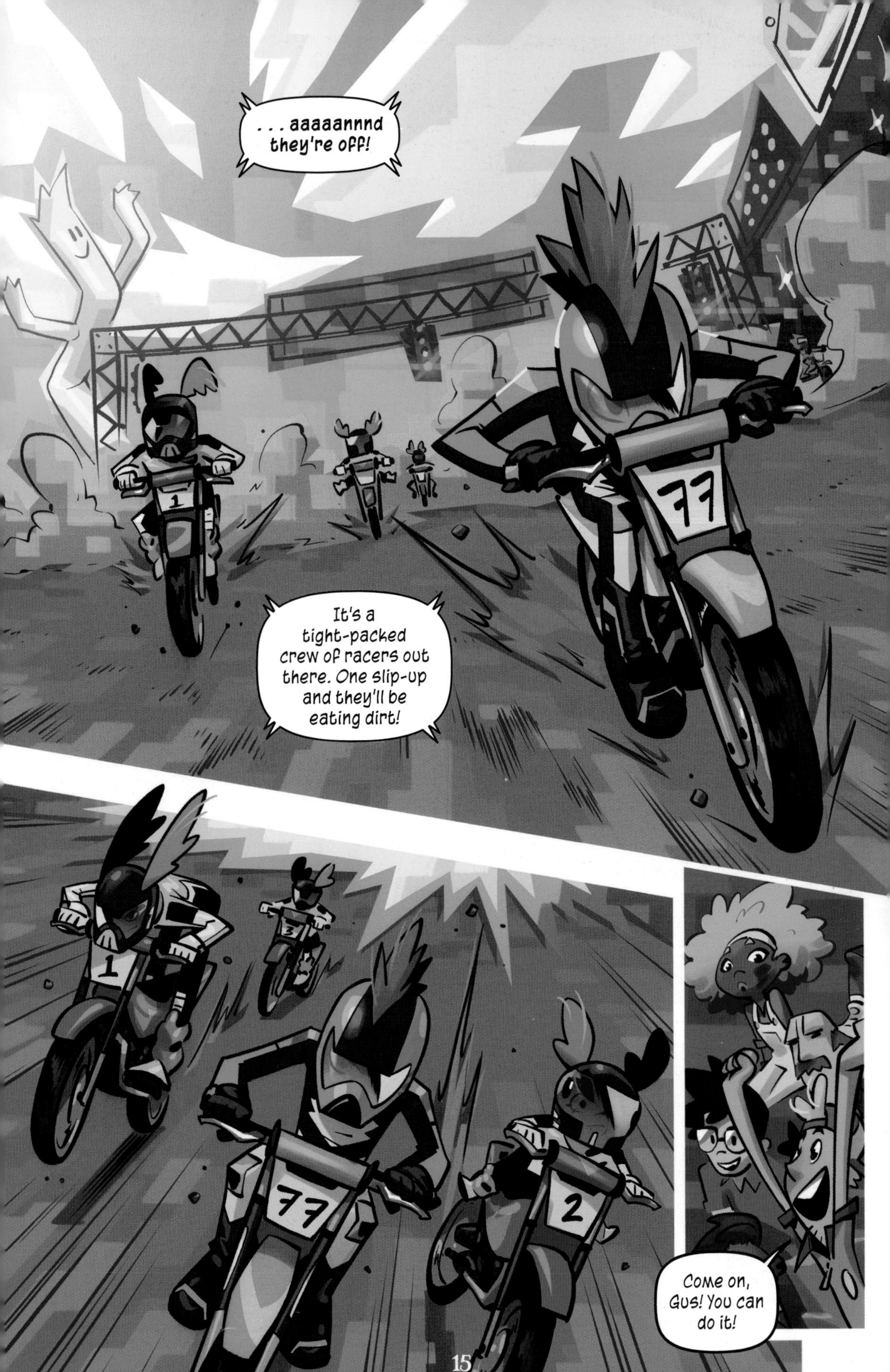
. . . aaaaannnd they're off!
It's a tight-packed crew of racers out there. One slip-up and they'll be eating dirt!
Come on, Gus! You can do it!

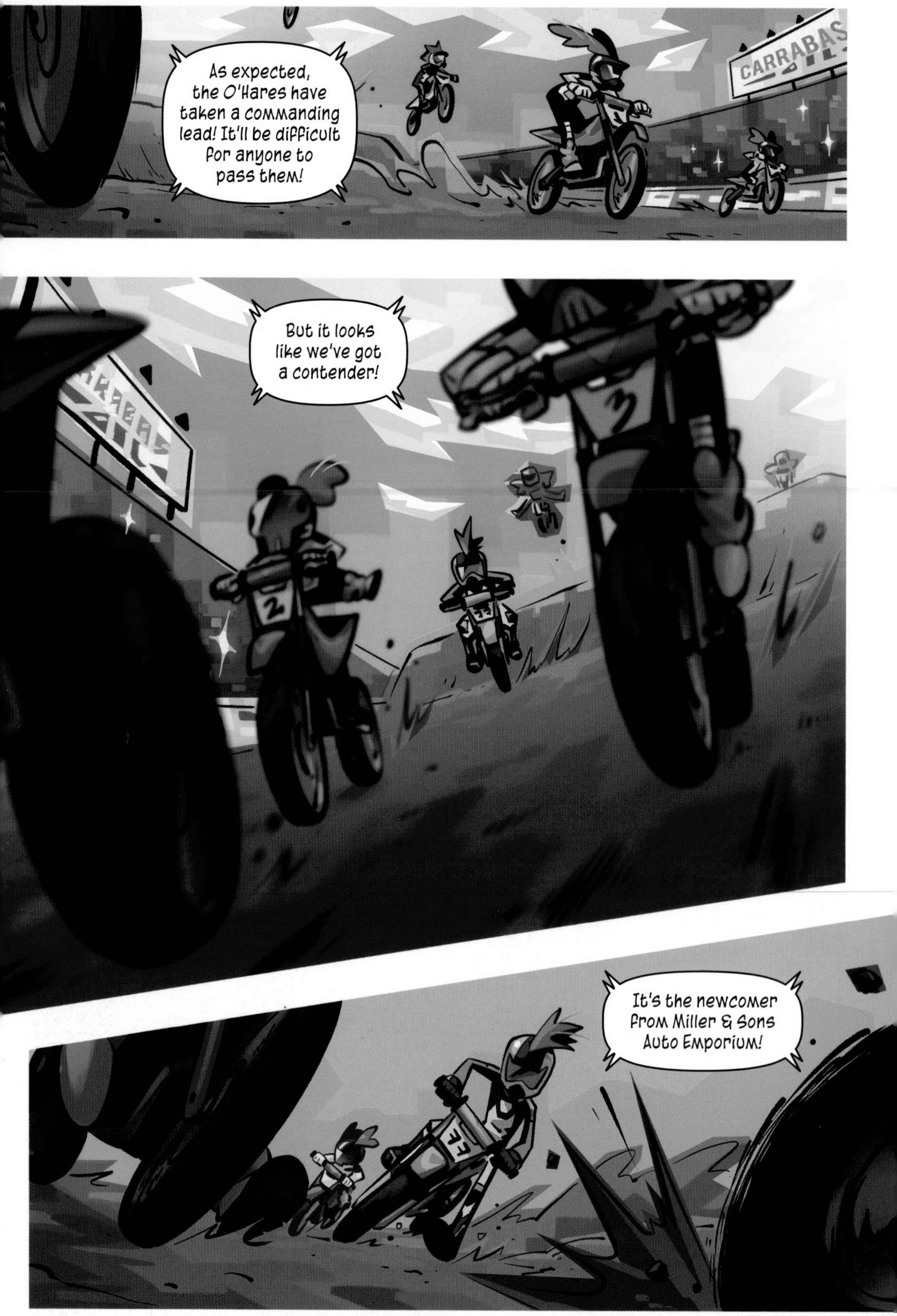
As expected, the O'Hares have taken a commanding lead! It'll be difficult for anyone to pass them!
CARRABAS
But it looks like we've got a contender!
It's the newcomer from Miller & Sons Auto Emporium!

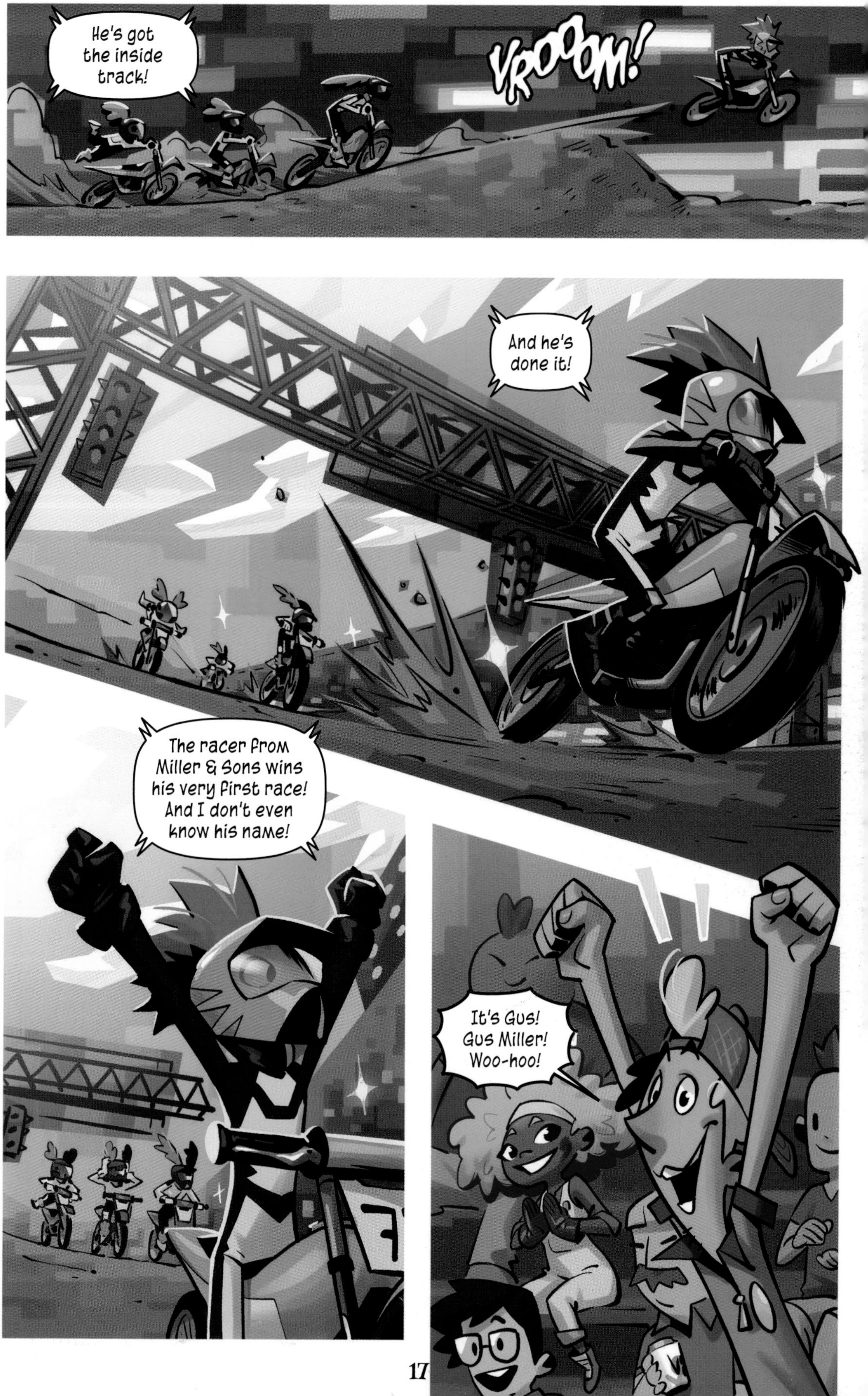
He's got the inside track!
VROOOM!
And he's done it!
The racer from Miller & Sons wins his very first race! And I don't even know his name!
It's Gus! Gus Miller! Woo-hoo!

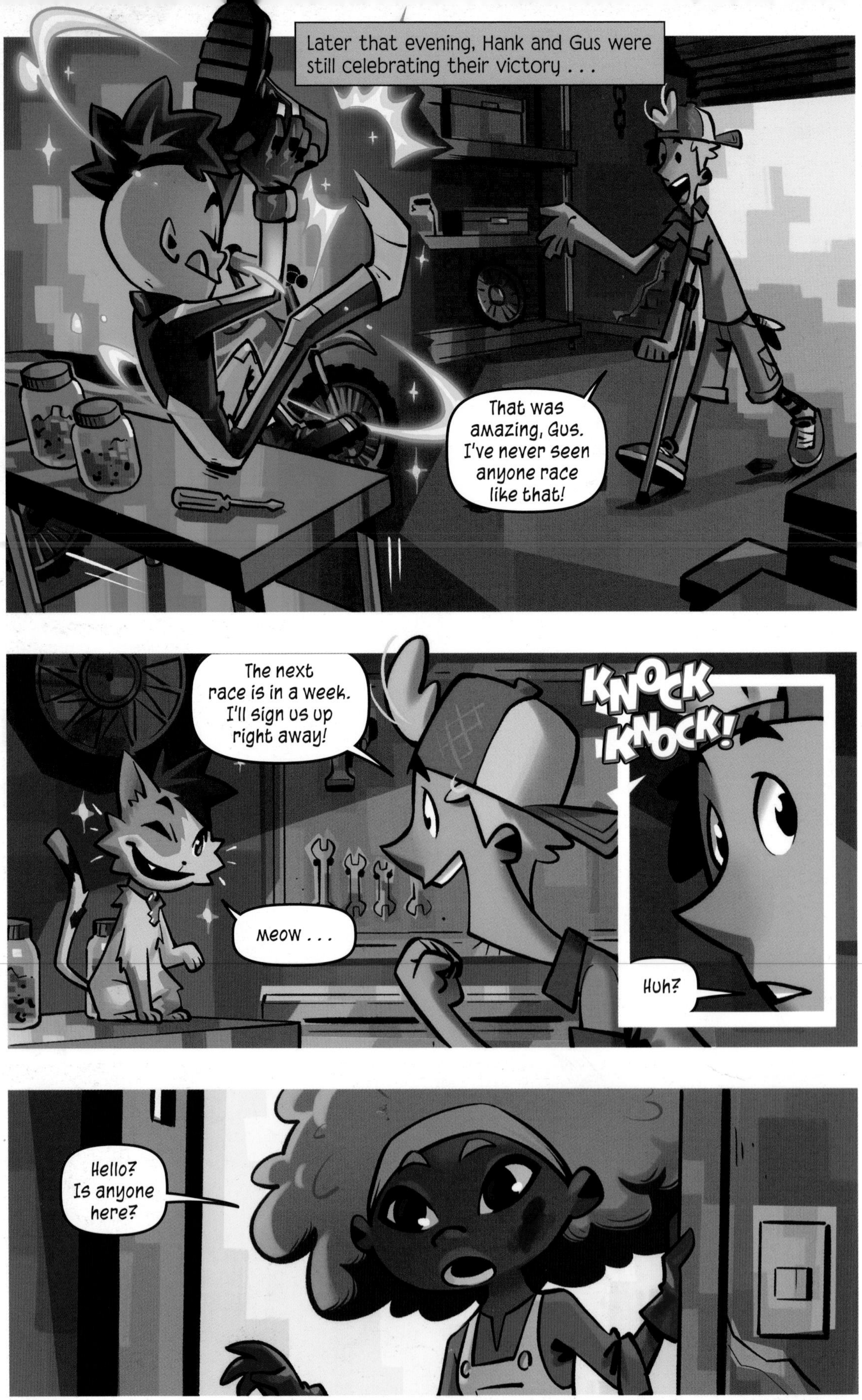
Later that evening, Hank and Gus were still celebrating their victory . . .
That was amazing, Gus. I've never seen anyone race like that!
The next race is in a week. I'll sign us up right away!
Meow . . .
KNOCK KNOCK!
Huh?
Hello? Is anyone here?

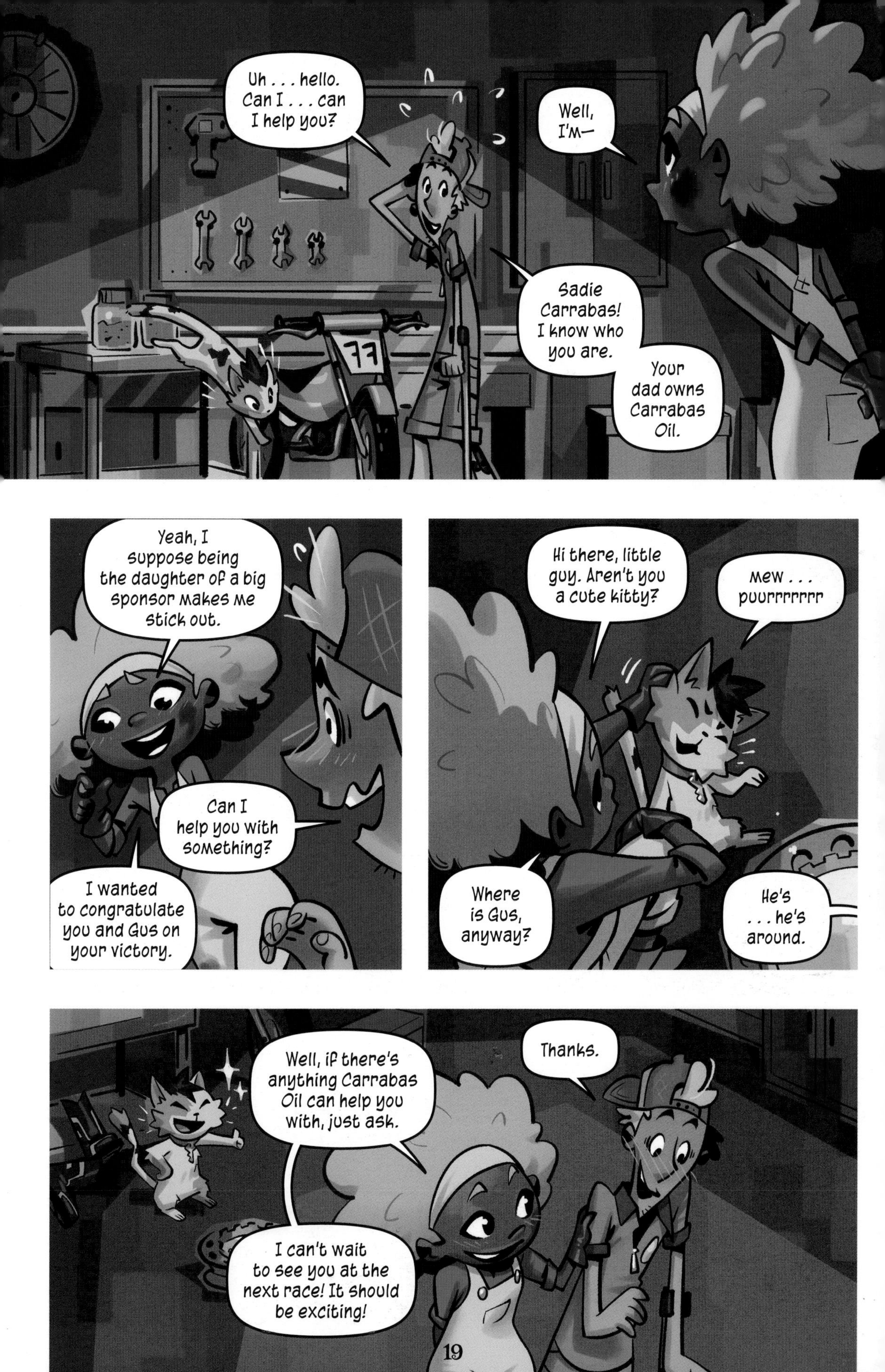
Uh . . . hello. Can I . . . can I help you?
Well, I'm—
Sadie Carrabas! I know who you are.
Your dad owns Carrabas Oil.
Yeah, I suppose being the daughter of a big sponsor makes me stick out.
Can I help you with something?
I wanted to congratulate you and Gus on your victory.
Hi there, little guy. Aren't you a cute kitty?
Mew . . . puurrrrrrr
Where is Gus, anyway?
He's . . . he's around.
Well, if there's anything Carrabas Oil can help you with, just ask.
Thanks.
I can't wait to see you at the next race! It should be exciting!

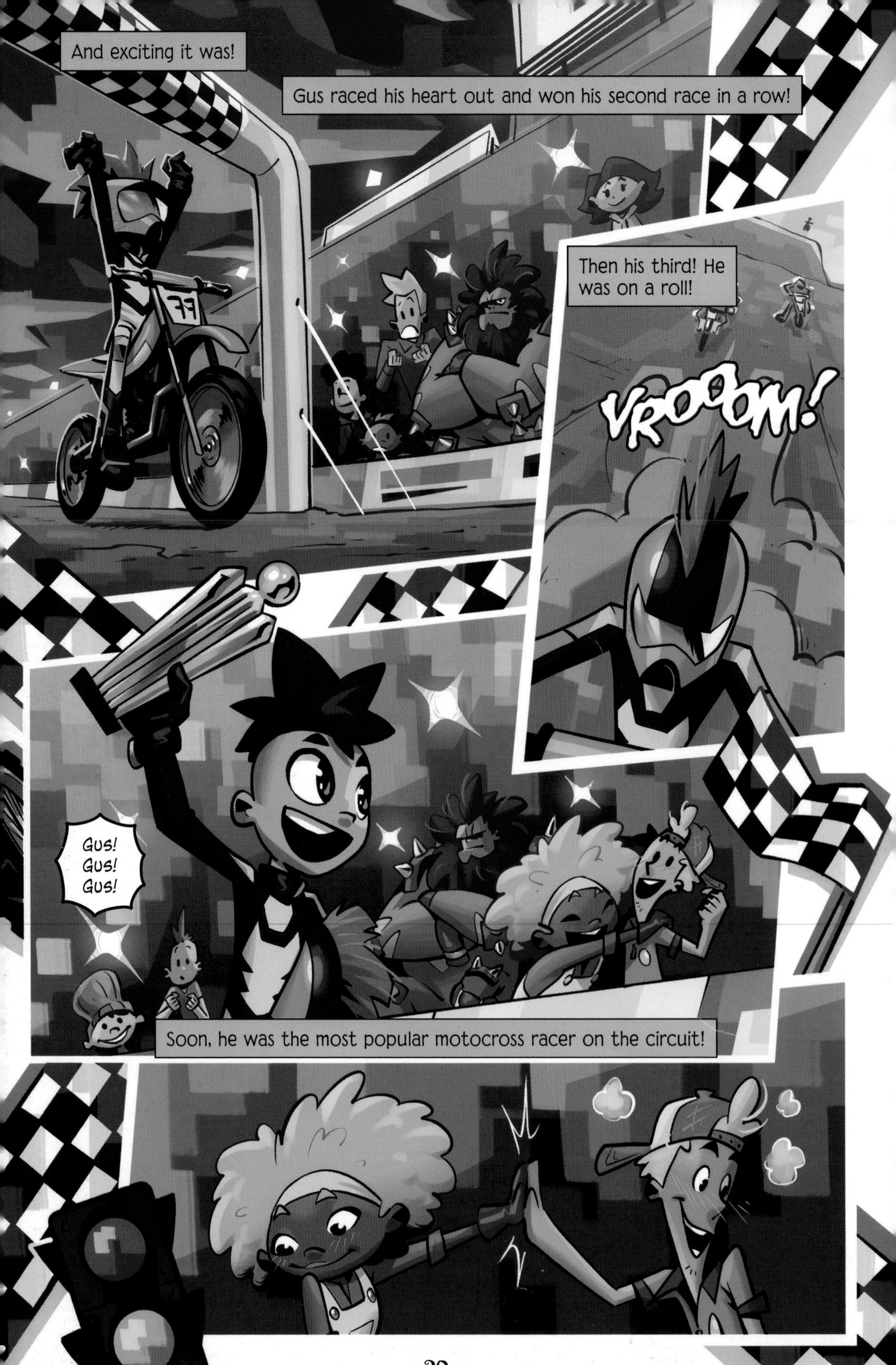
And exciting it was!
Gus raced his heart out and won his second race in a row!
Then his third! He was on a roll!
VROOOOM!
GUS! GUS! GUS!
Soon, he was the most popular motocross racer on the circuit!

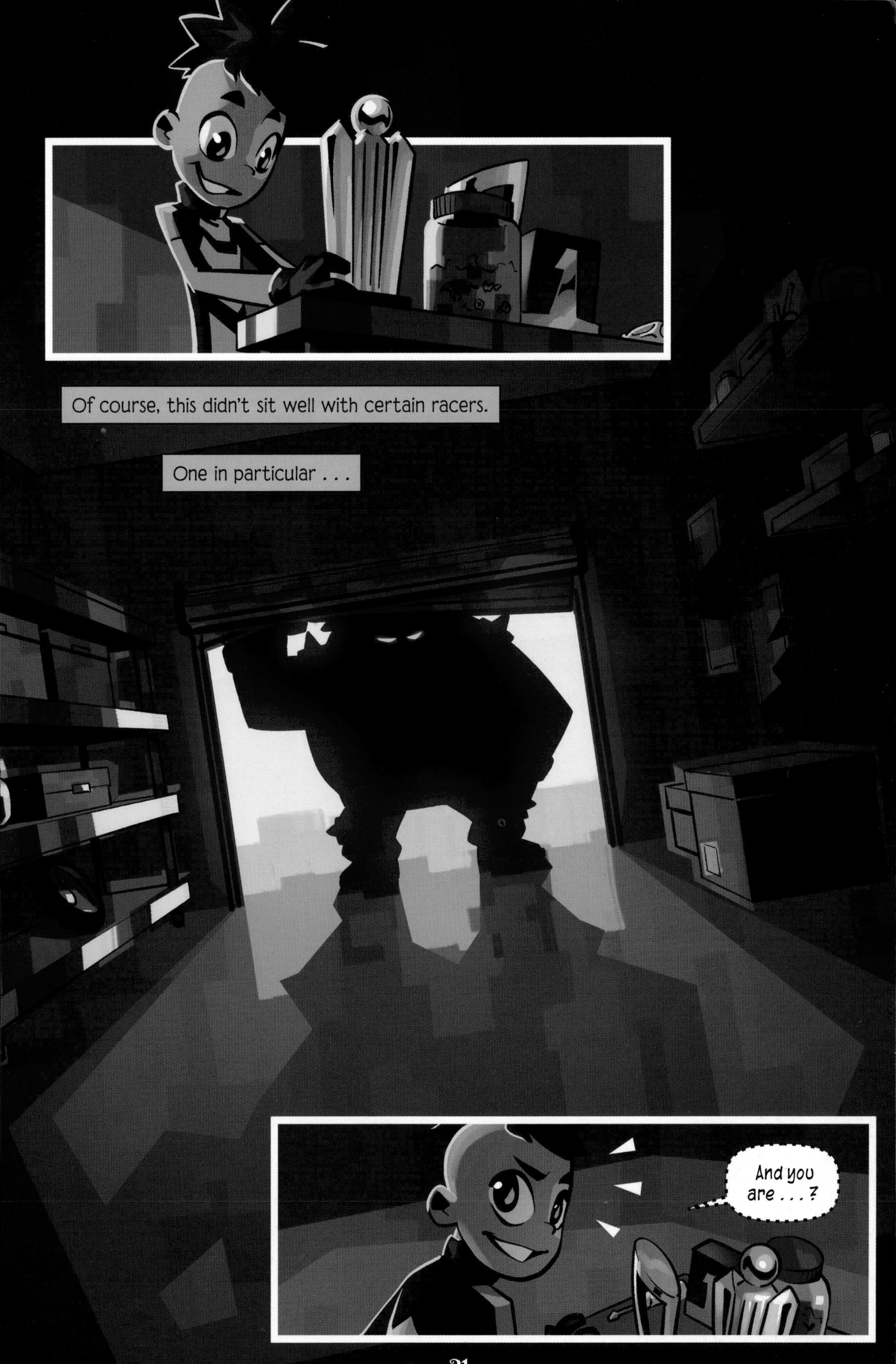
Of course, this didn't sit well with certain racers.
One in particular . . .
And you are . . . ?

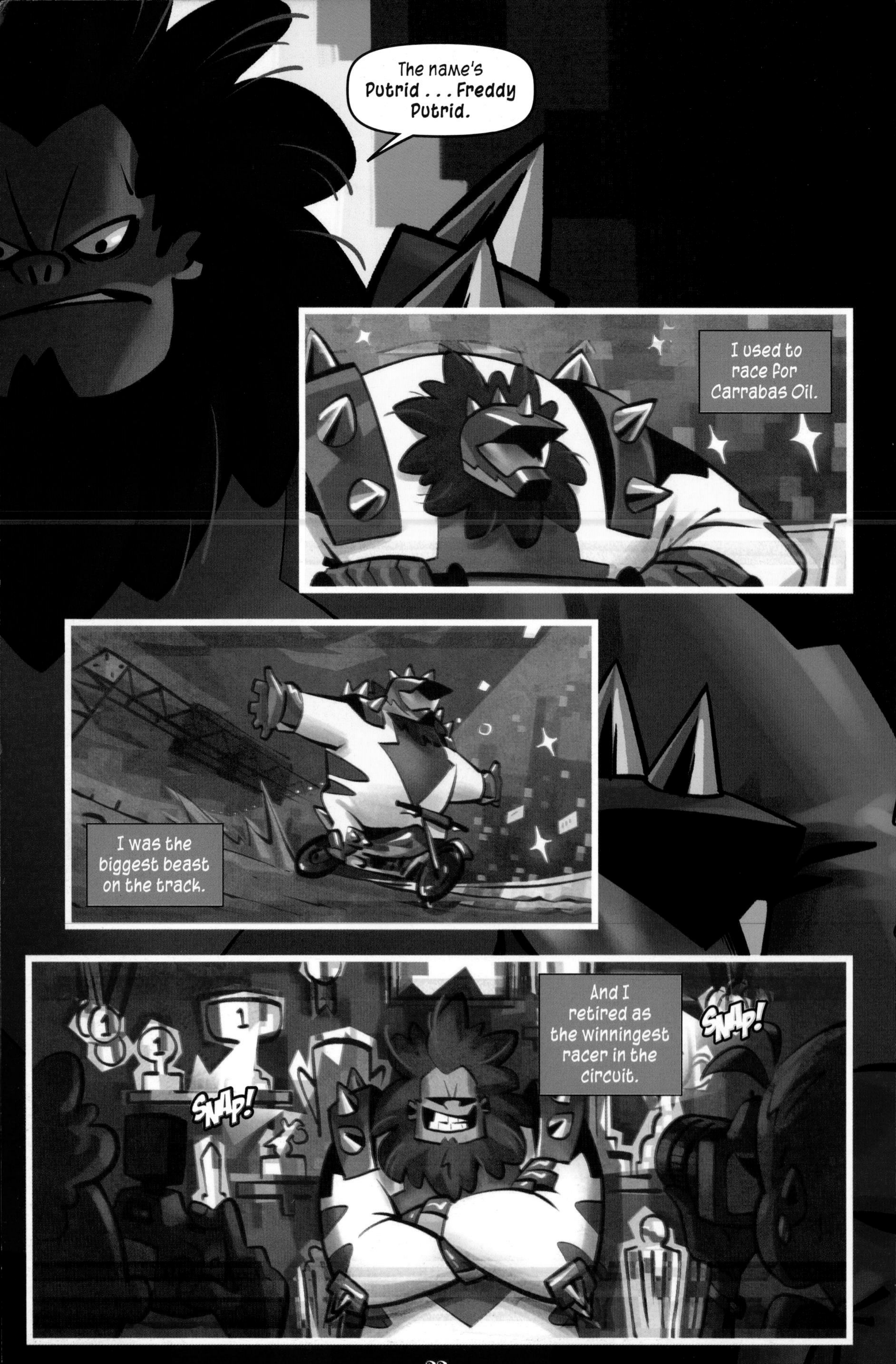

The name's Putrid . . . Freddy Putrid.
I used to race for Carrabas Oil.
I was the biggest beast on the track.
And I retired as the winningest racer in the circuit.
SNAP!
SNAP!

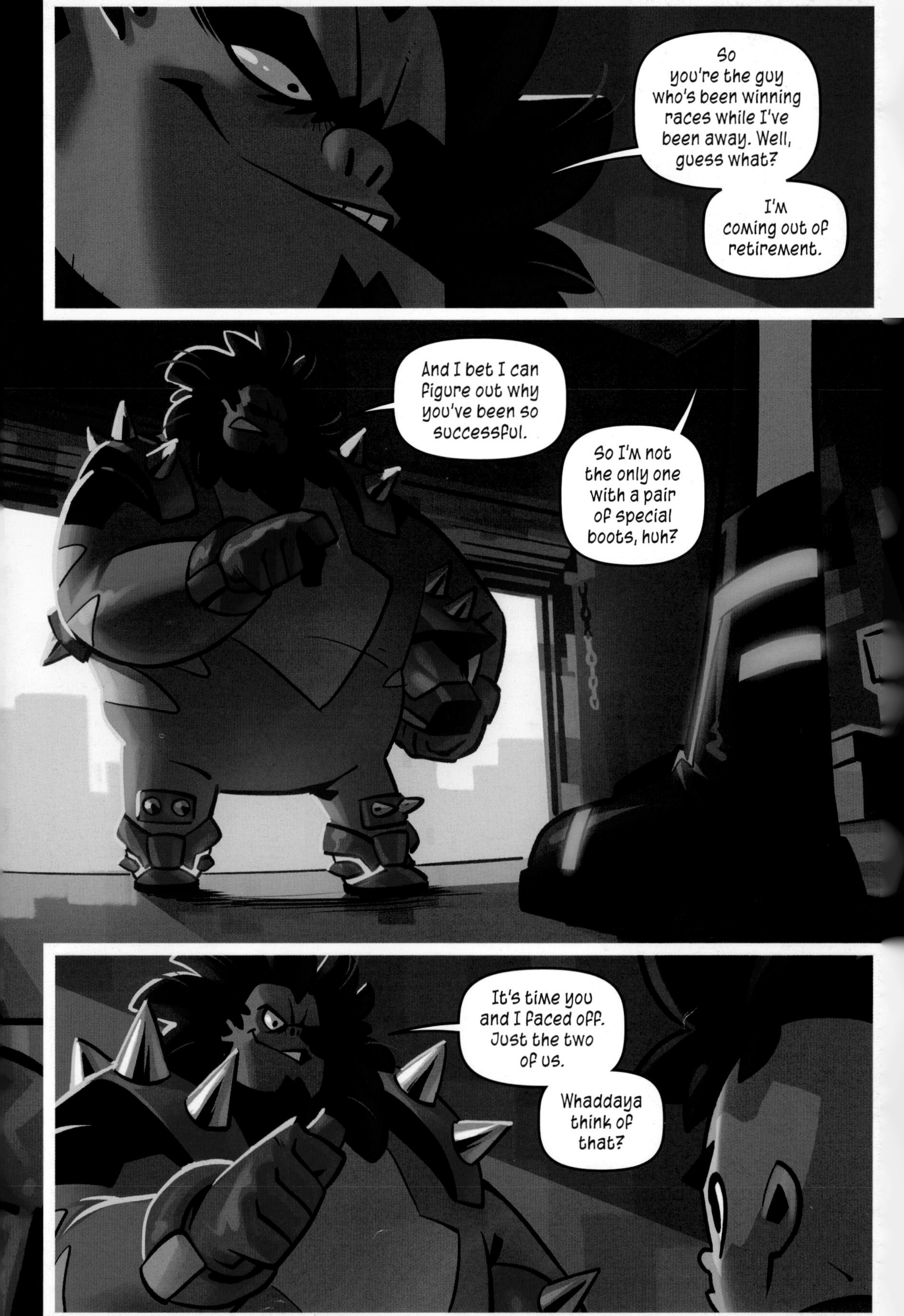
So you're the guy who's been winning races while I've been away. Well, guess what?
I'm coming out of retirement.
And I bet I can figure out why you've been so successful.
So I'm not the only one with a pair of special boots, huh?
It's time you and I faced off. Just the two of us.
Whaddaya think of that?

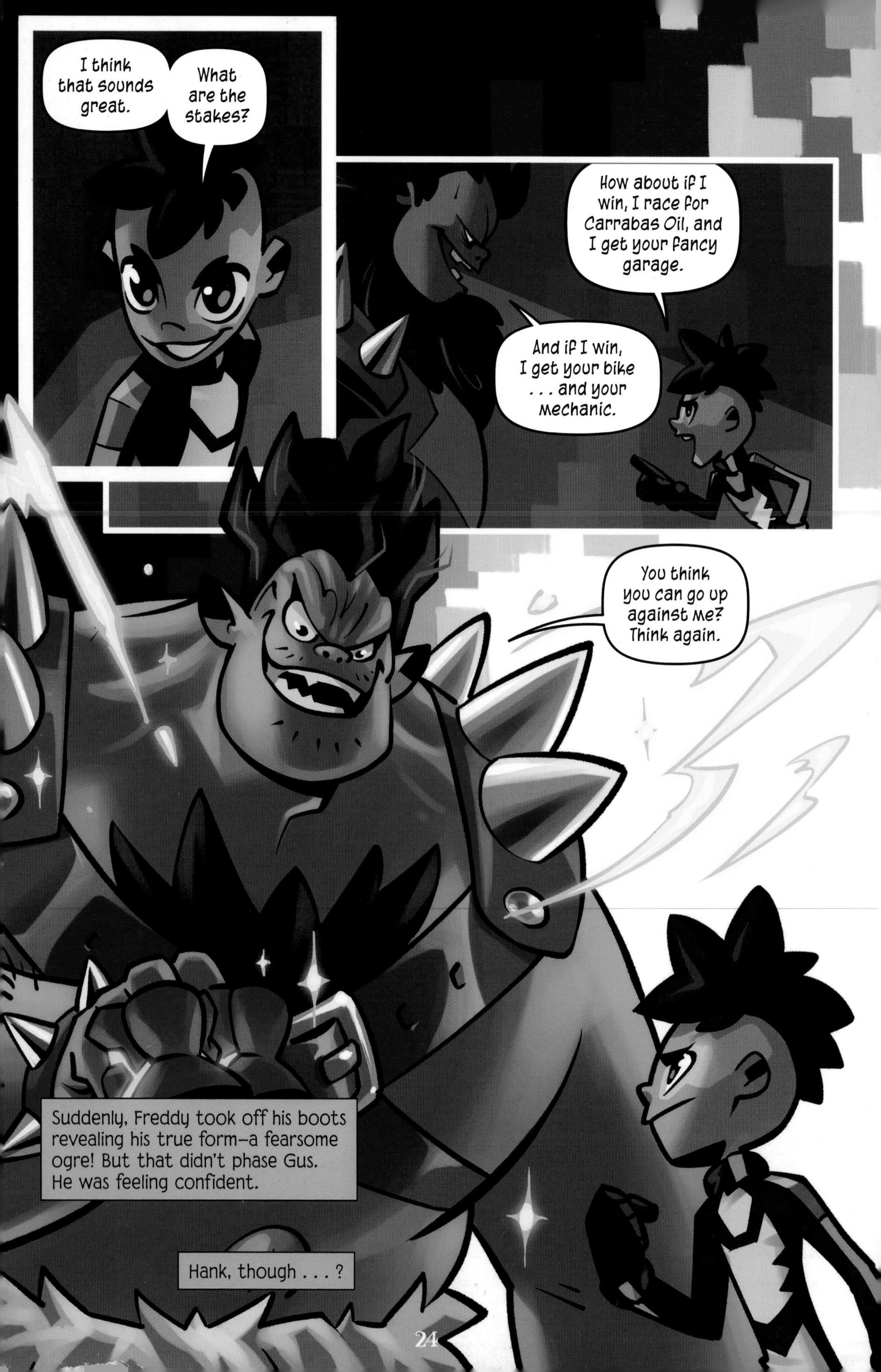
I think that sounds great.
What are the stakes?
How about if I win, I race for Carrabas Oil, and I get your fancy garage.
And if I win, I get your bike . . . and your mechanic.
You think you can go up against me? Think again.
Suddenly, Freddy took off his boots revealing his true form—a fearsome ogre! But that didn't phase Gus. He was feeling confident.
Hank, though . . . ?

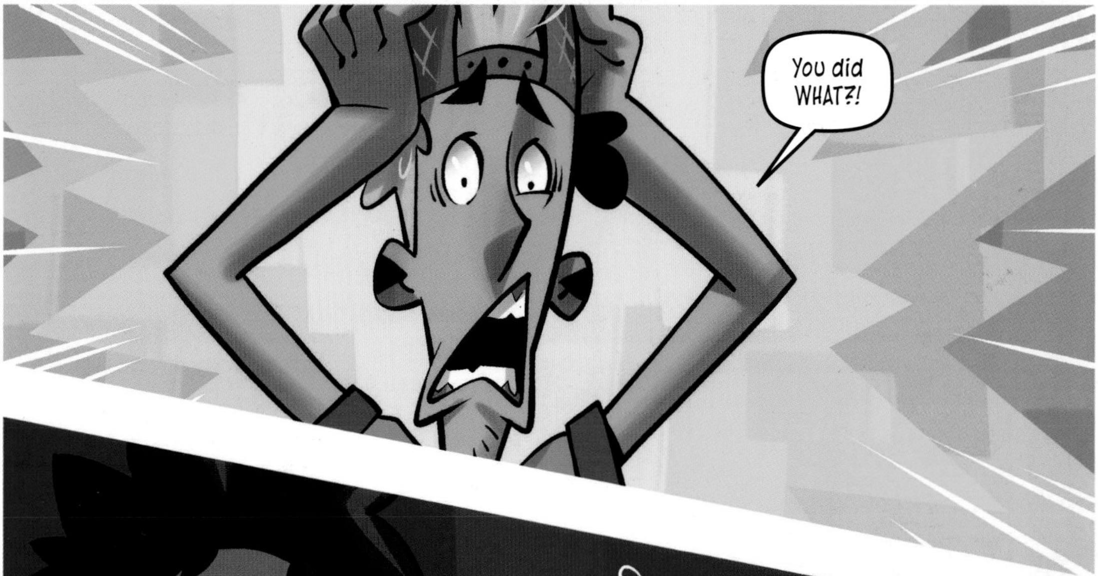
You did WHAT?!

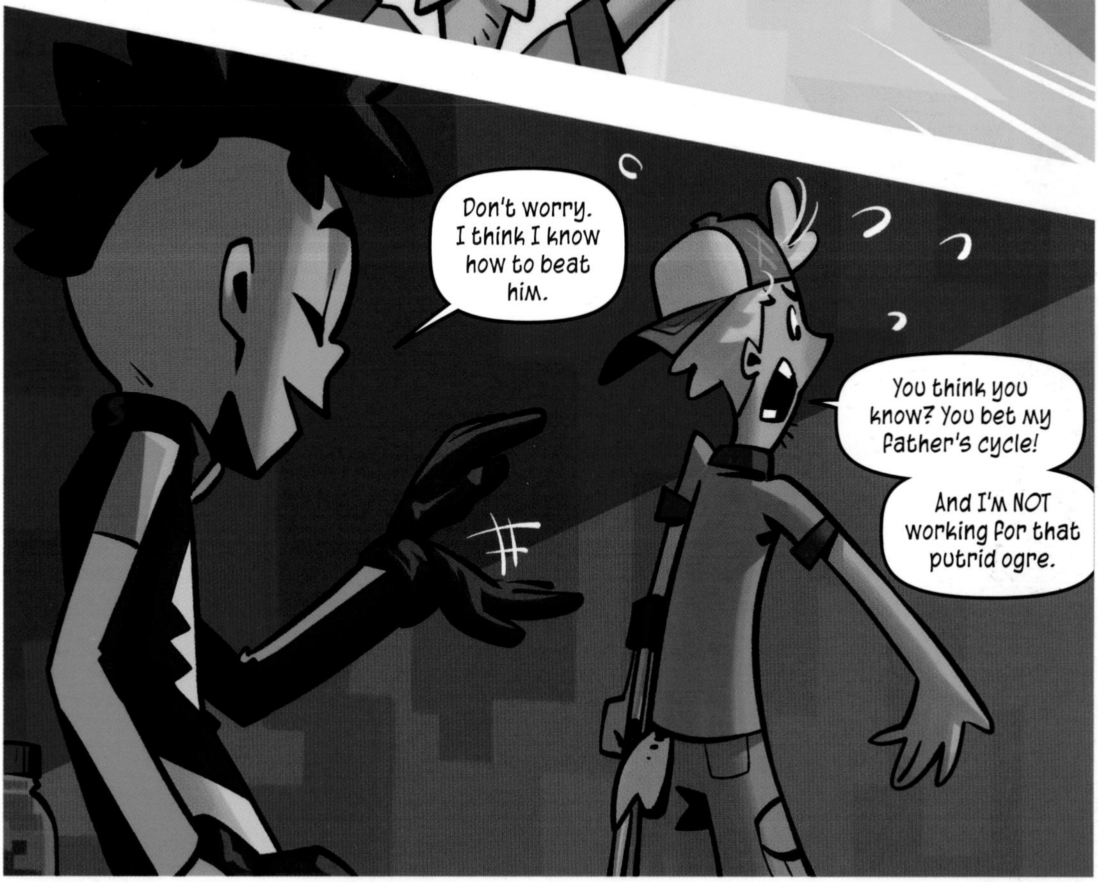
Don't worry. I think I know how to beat him.
You think you know? You bet my father's cycle!
And I'M NOT working for that putrid ogre.

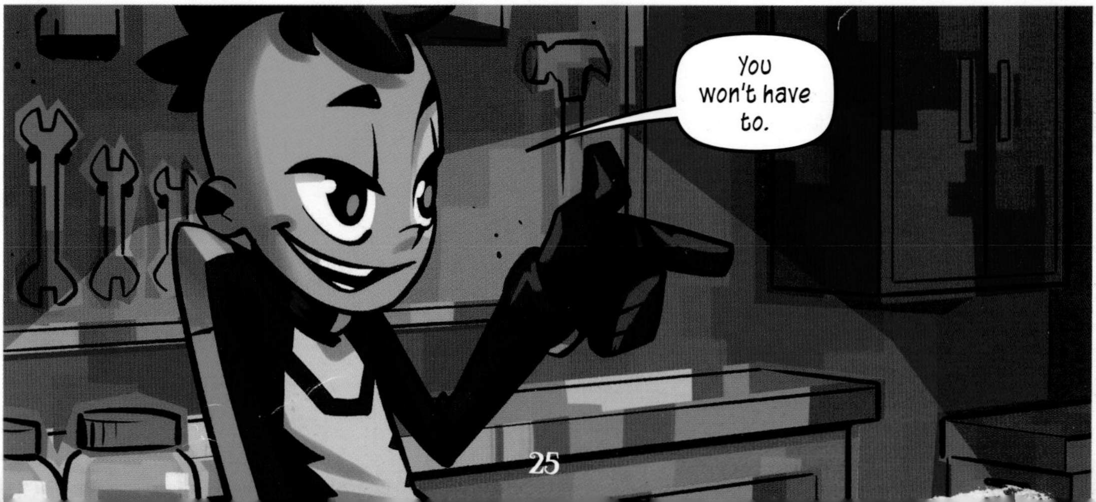
You won't have to.

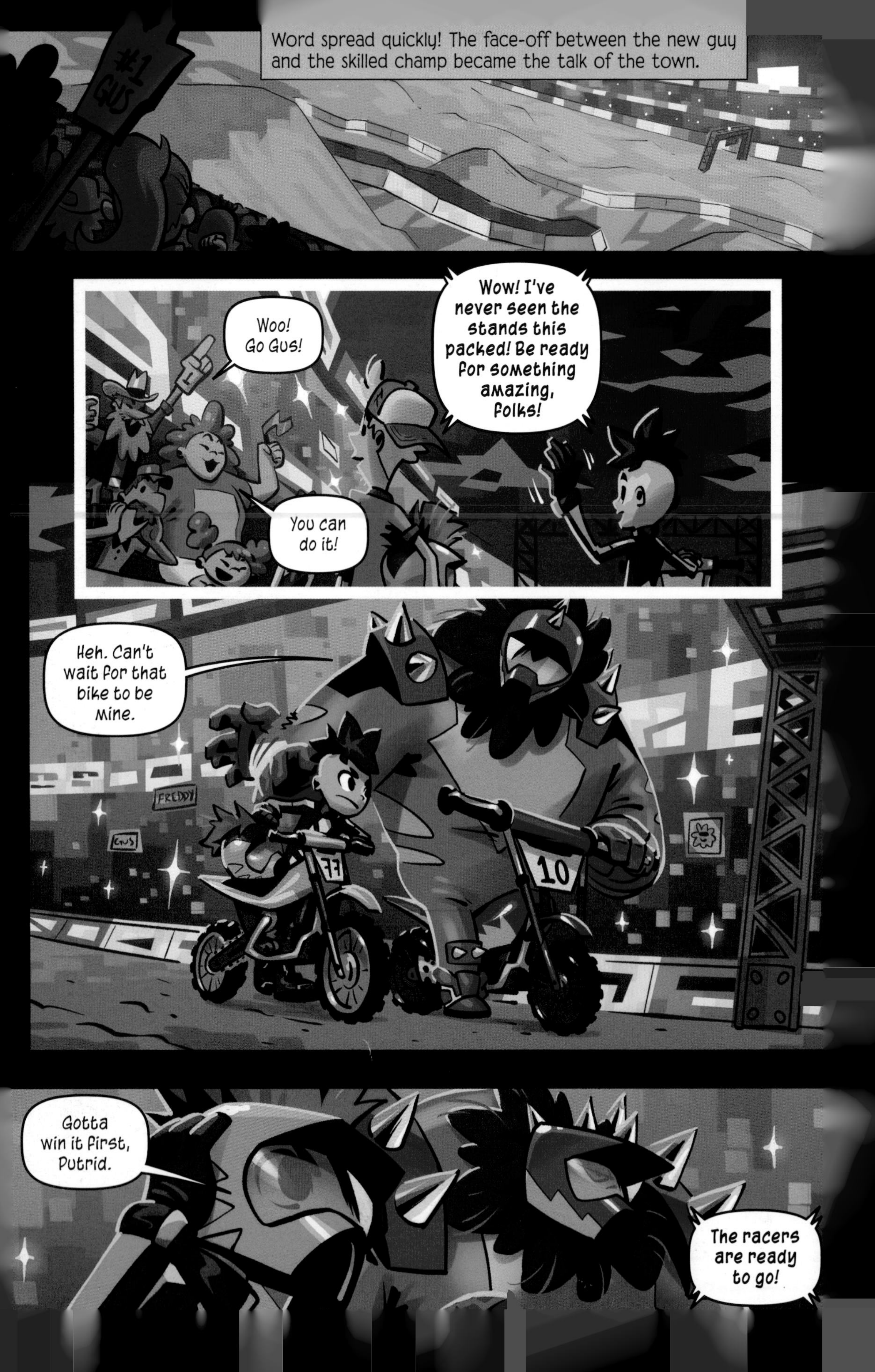
Word spread quickly! The face-off between the new guy and the skilled champ became the talk of the town.
#1 GUS
Woo! Go Gus!
Wow! I've never seen the stands this packed! Be ready for something amazing, folks!
You can do it!
Heh. Can't wait for that bike to be mine.
FREDDY
GUS
77
10
Gotta win it first, Putrid.
The racers are ready to go!

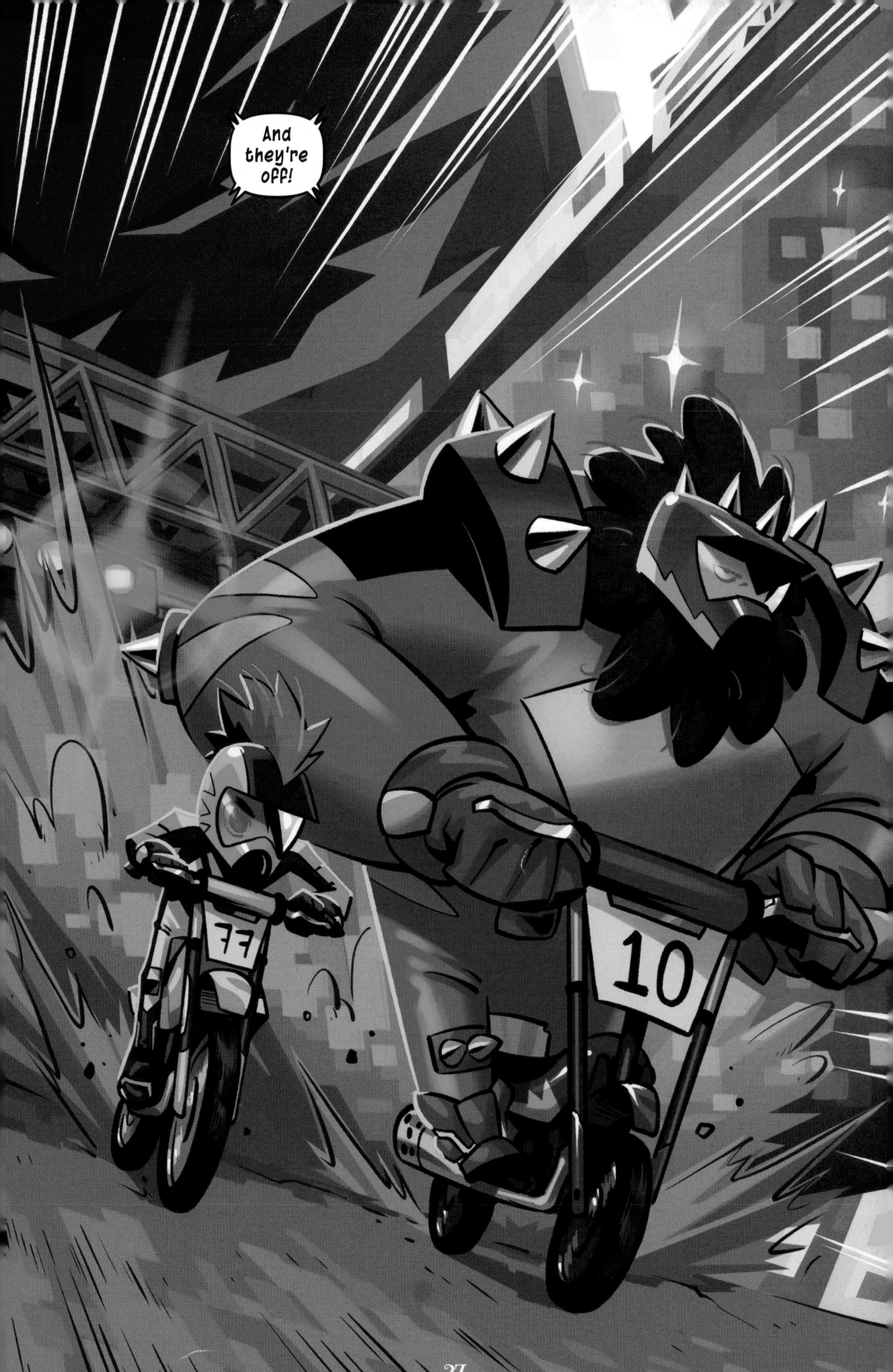
And they're off!
77
10

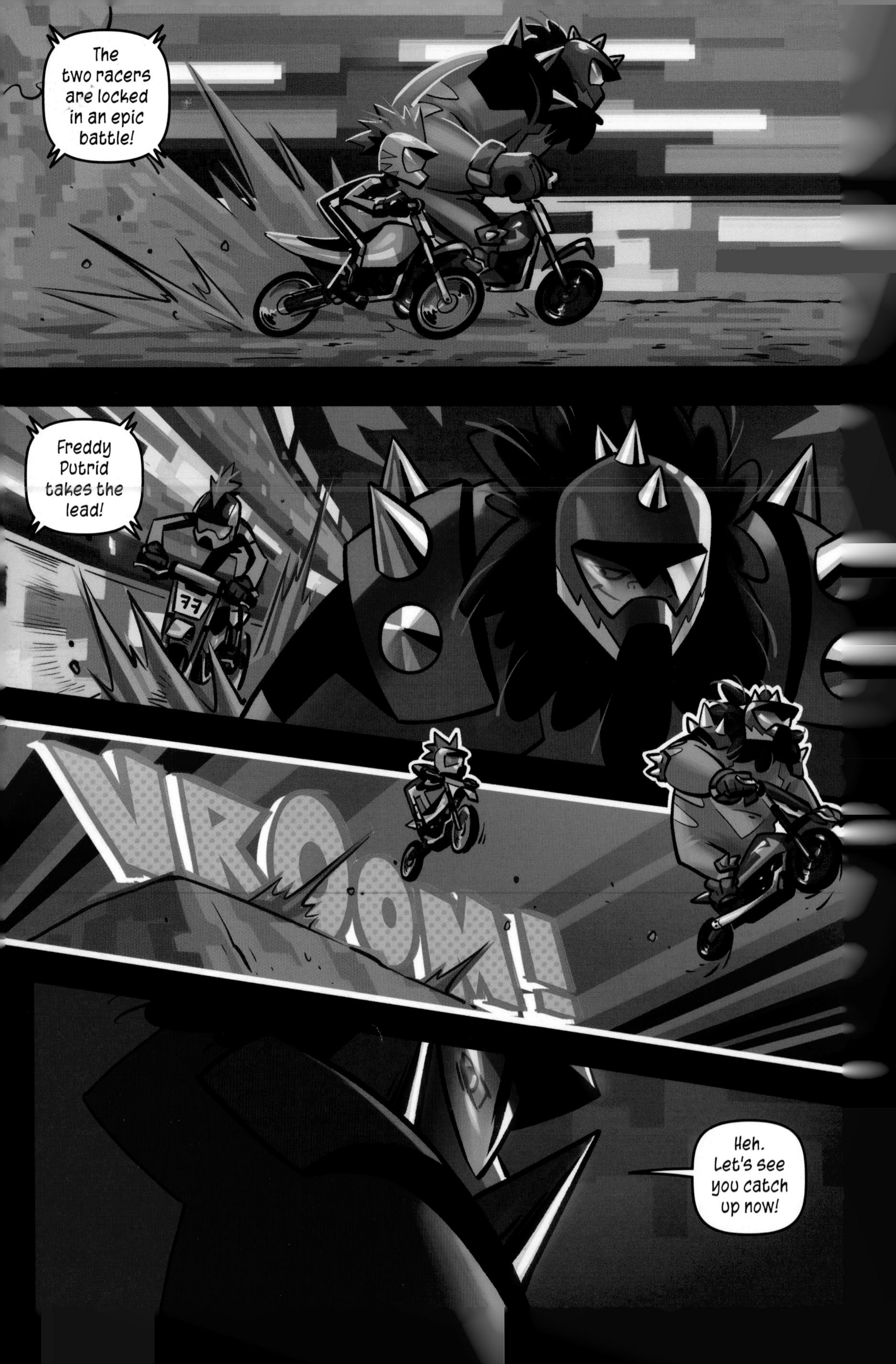
The two racers are locked in an epic battle!
Freddy Putrid takes the lead!
77
VROOM!
Heh. Let's see you catch up now!

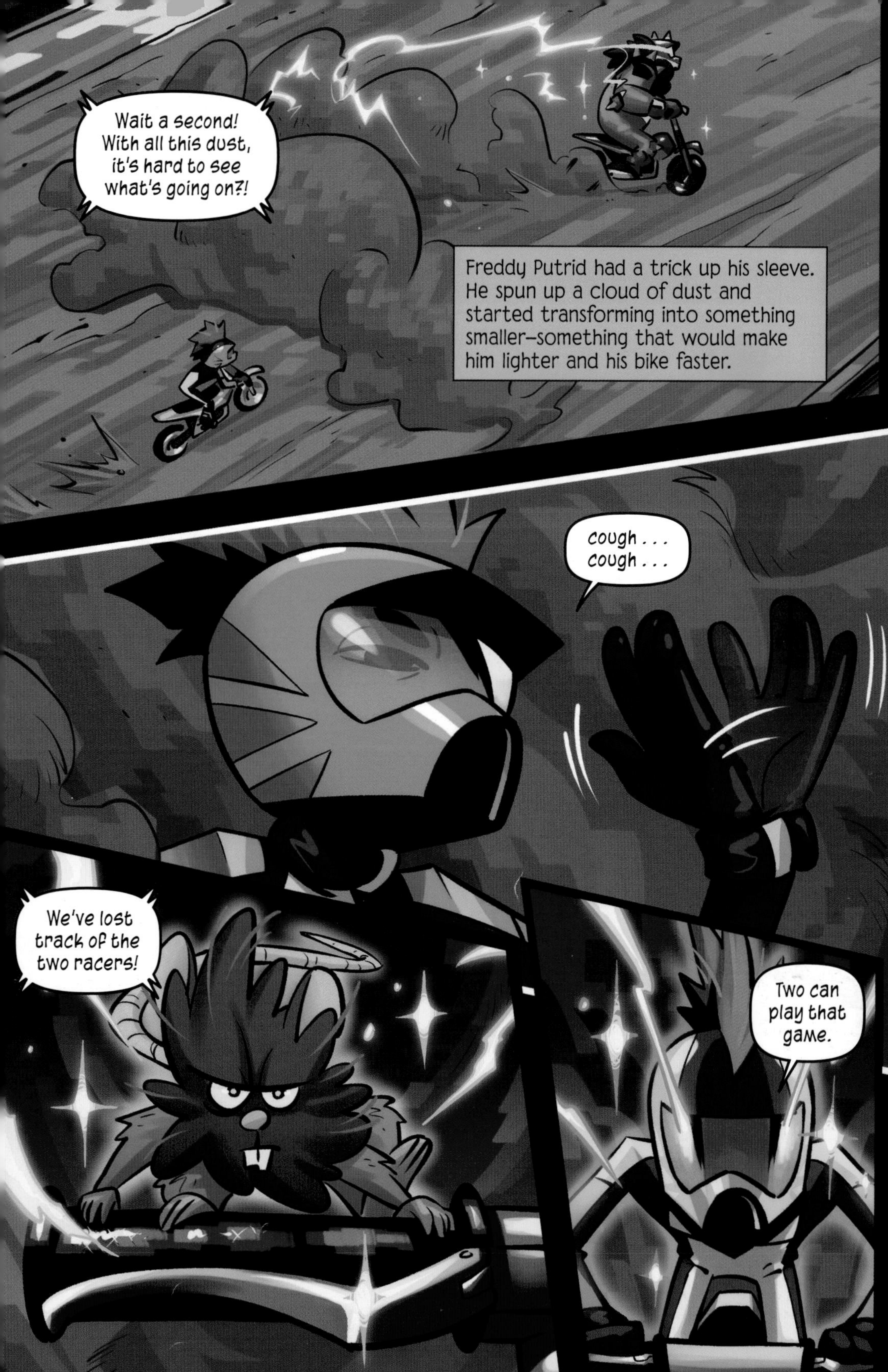
Wait a second! With all this dust, it's hard to see what's going on?!
Freddy Putrid had a trick up his sleeve. He spun up a cloud of dust and started transforming into something smaller—something that would make him lighter and his bike faster.
cough . . . cough . . .
We've lost track of the two racers!
Two can play that game.

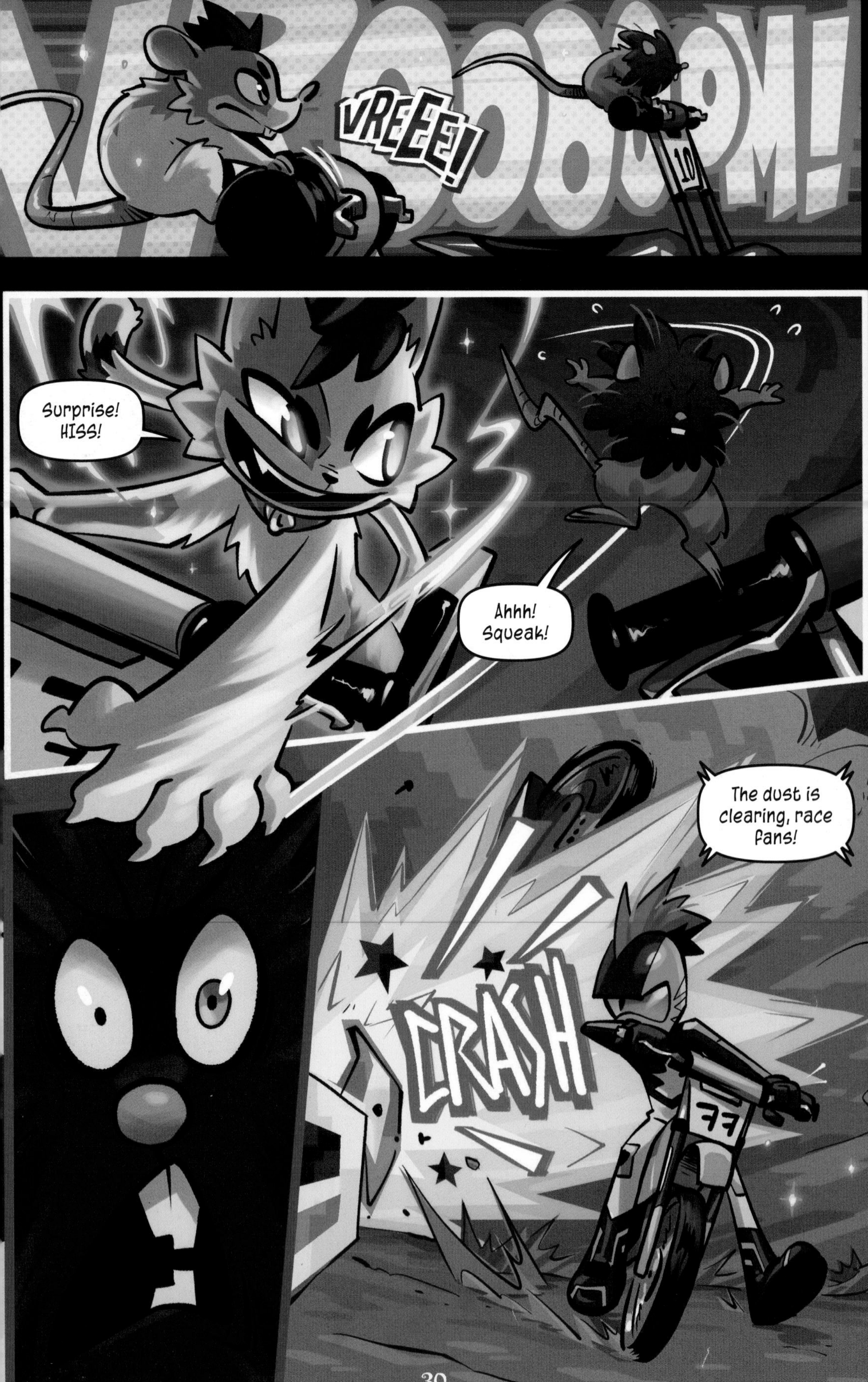
VREEE!
Surprise! HISS!
Ahhh! Squeak!
The dust is clearing, race fans!
CRASH

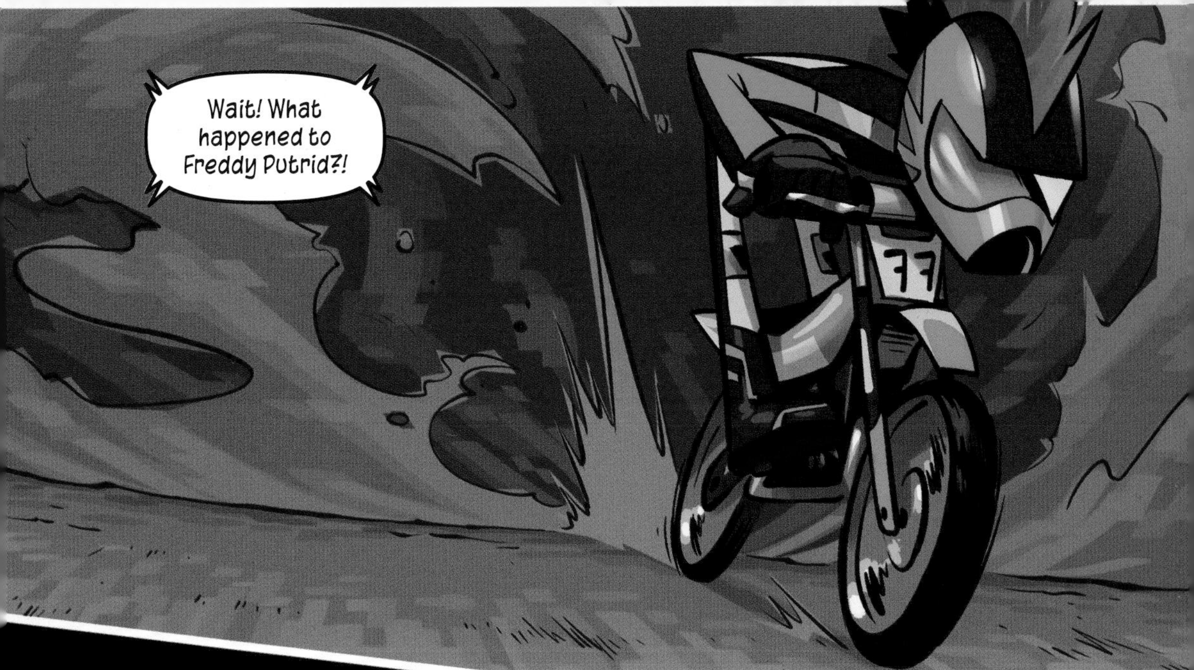

Wait! What happened to Freddy Putrid?!

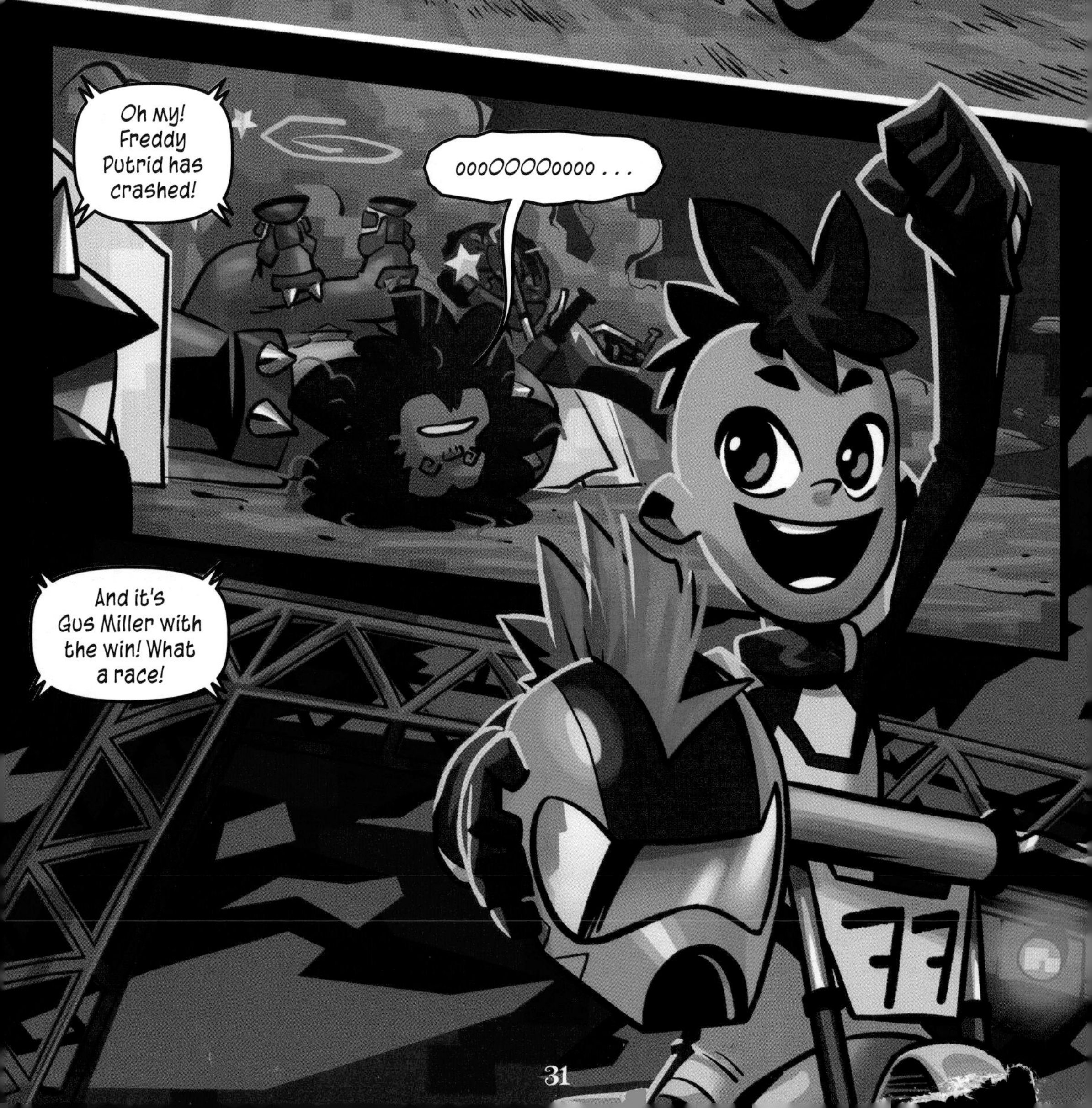

Oh my! Freddy Putrid has crashed!
oooOOOOoooo . . .
And it's Gus Miller with the win! What a race!
77

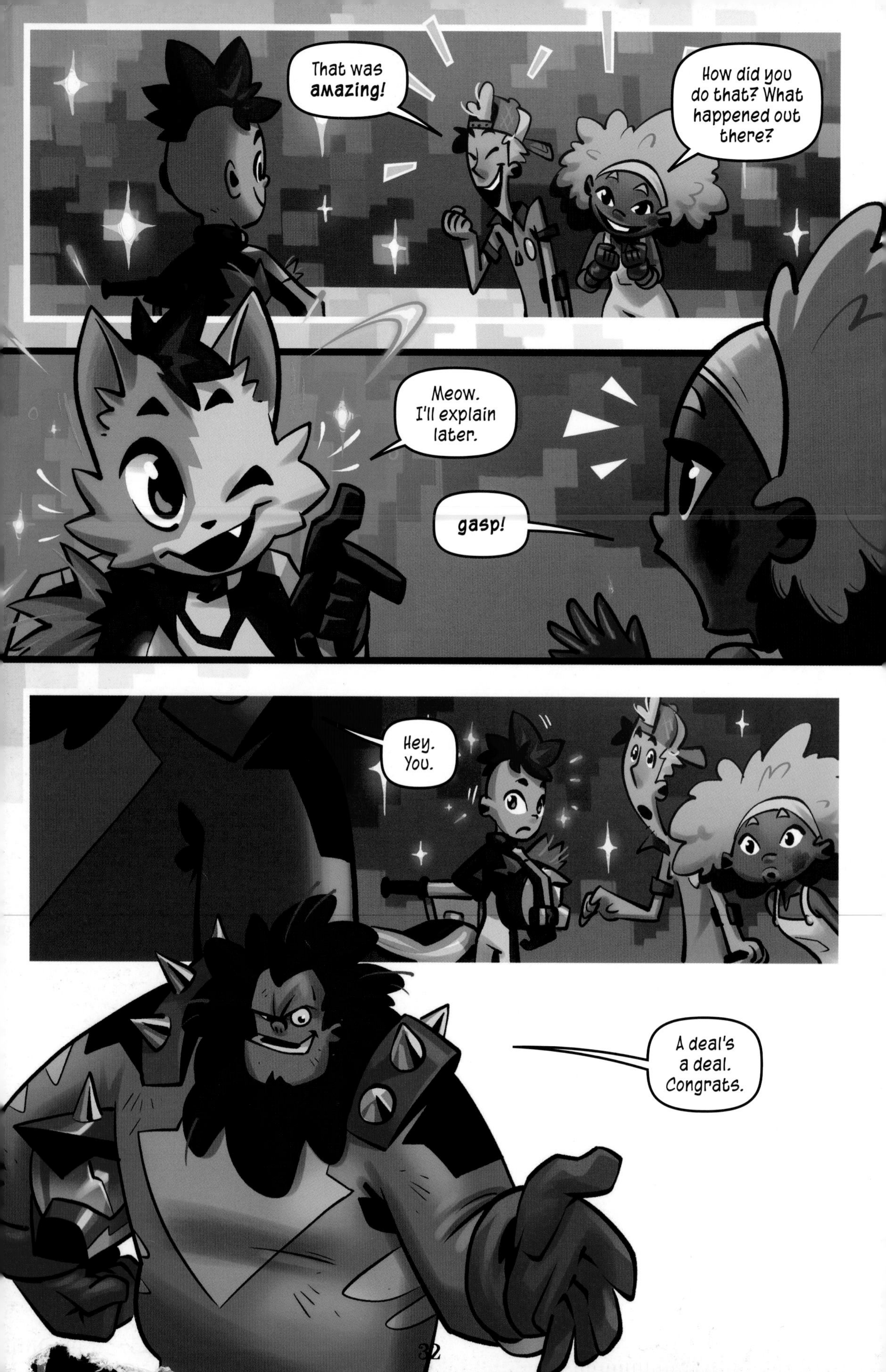
That was amazing!
How did you do that? What happened out there?
Meow. I'll explain later.
gasp!
Hey. You.
A deal's a deal. Congrats.

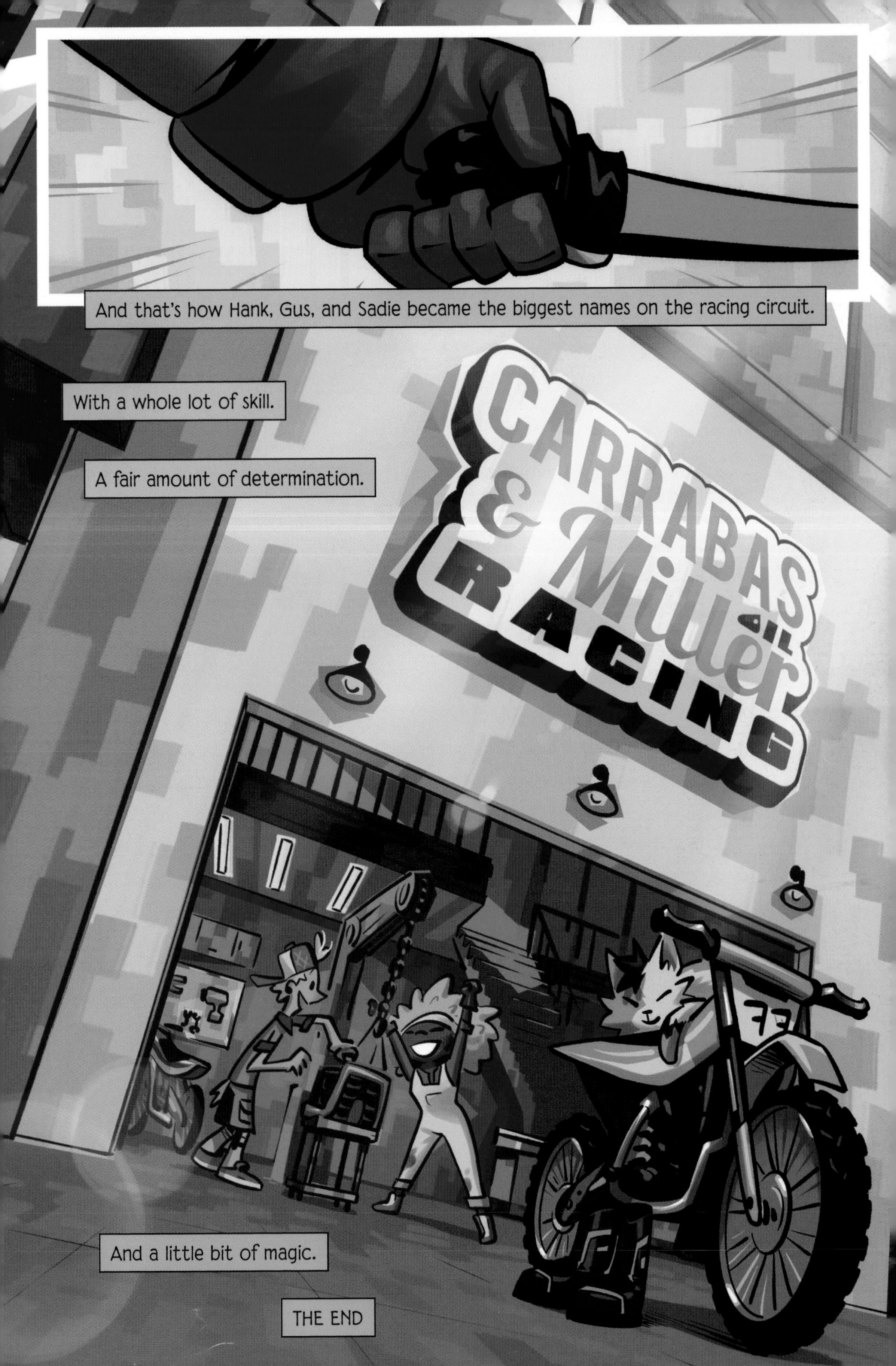
And that's how Hank, Gus, and Sadie became the biggest names on the racing circuit.
With a whole lot of skill.
A fair amount of determination.
CARRABAS & Miller RACING
And a little bit of magic.
THE END

ALL ABOUT THE ORIGINAL TALE!

The original version of Puss in Boots doesn't have dangerous motocross races—but it does have a tricky talking cat!

The most well-known version of Puss in Boots dates back to the 1600s and was written by French author Charles Perrault. In the story, a miller dies and leaves his three sons his mill, his donkey, and his cat. The youngest son, being his favorite, is given the cat. The youngest son discovers the cat can speak, and the cat vows to help the son make a living for himself if the son will buy her a pair of boots and a large bag.

The cat uses the boots and bag to magically catch rabbits for dinner. Then, upon catching more, she delivers the rabbits to the king and offers them as a gift. She does this several times, earning the king's favor and the favor of his daughter. He tells the king about his owner and says he is a prince.

At this same time, an ogre has been eating children and terrifying the people of the land. The cat confronts the ogre, saying, "Great ogre! I hear that you are so clever you can turn into any creature you please!" The cat dares him to turn into a mouse. The ogre accepts the dare, and the cat promptly kills him.

With the ogre gone, his castle is up for grabs. The cat and the miller's son take it as their own. Then the cat invites the king and his daughter to a great feast. The king is delighted and offers his daughter as a bride for the miller's son. A grand wedding is held, and the poor miller's son, thanks to his talking cat, becomes a prince.

A FAR OUT GUIDE TO THE TALE'S MYSTERY TWISTS!

In the original story, the miller's son is simply given a cat. Here, he's given a cat, a motocross bike, and a pair of magical boots!

In the original, Puss uses the boots and bag to capture rabbits. In the new story, Gus uses them to out-race competitors on the motocross track!

In the first story, the Ogre lives in a castle and eats children. In this one he's a bully who races dirty and has his own pair of magical boots.

The miller's son in the original tale ends up as a prince. In this one he gets a racing partner and a sponsor!

VISUAL QUESTIONS

Graphic novels use art to tell the story. Some panels don't even need words. How are the two characters feeling in this panel? How do you know?

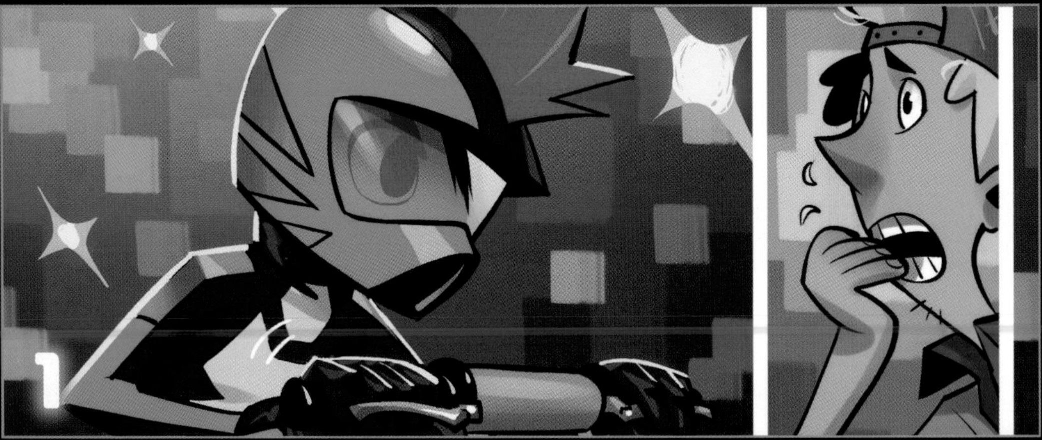
1

In graphic novels, the way word bubbles are drawn can give readers hints. Who is speaking on this spread? How do you know?

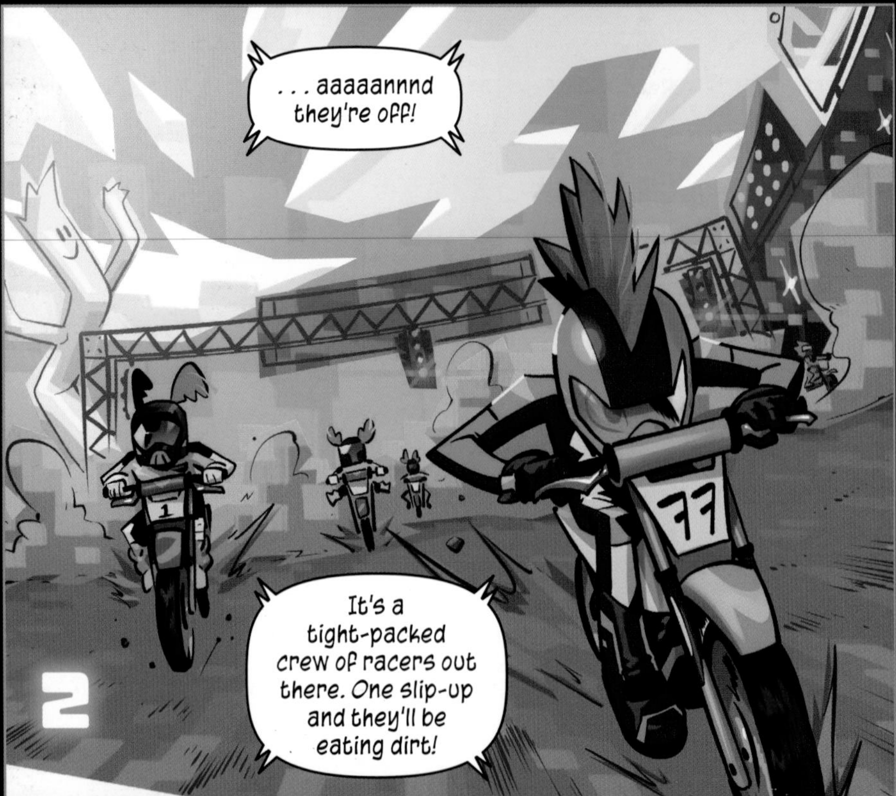
. . . aaaaannnd they're off!
1
77
It's a tight-packed crew of racers out there. One slip-up and they'll be eating dirt!
2

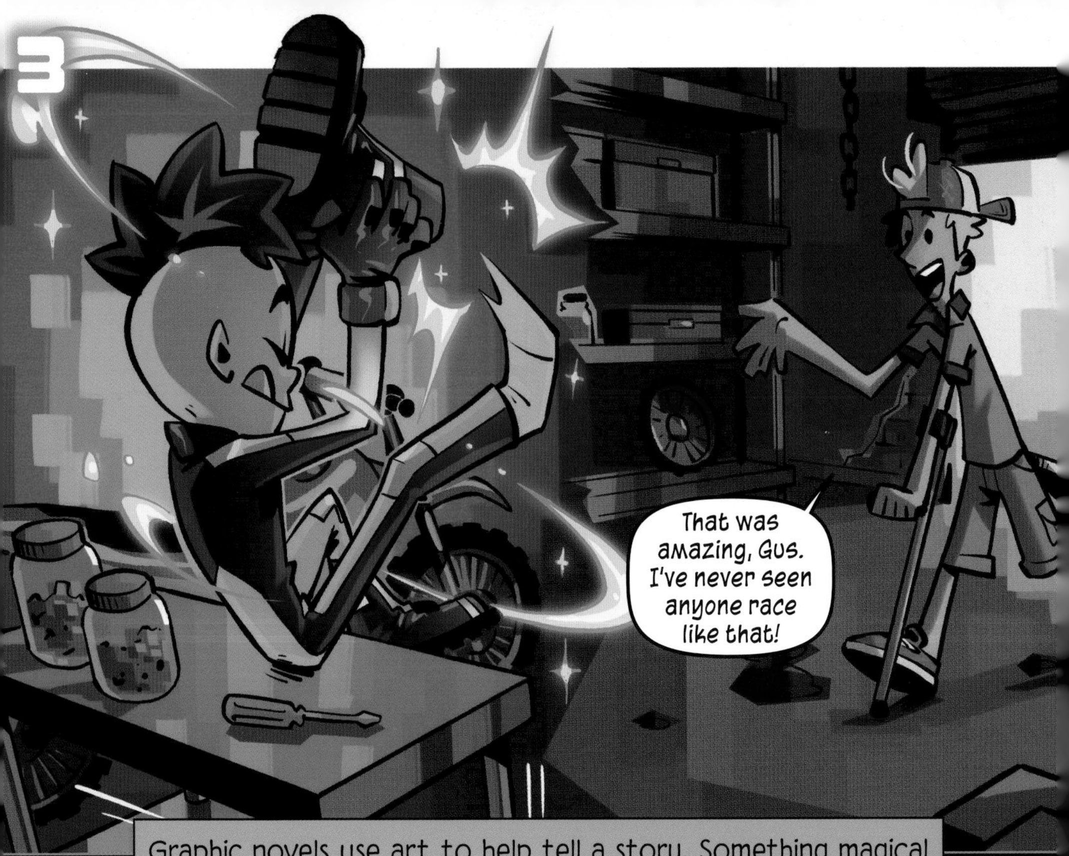
3
That was amazing, Gus. I've never seen anyone race like that!

Graphic novels use art to help tell a story. Something magical is happening in this panel. What clues help you know that?

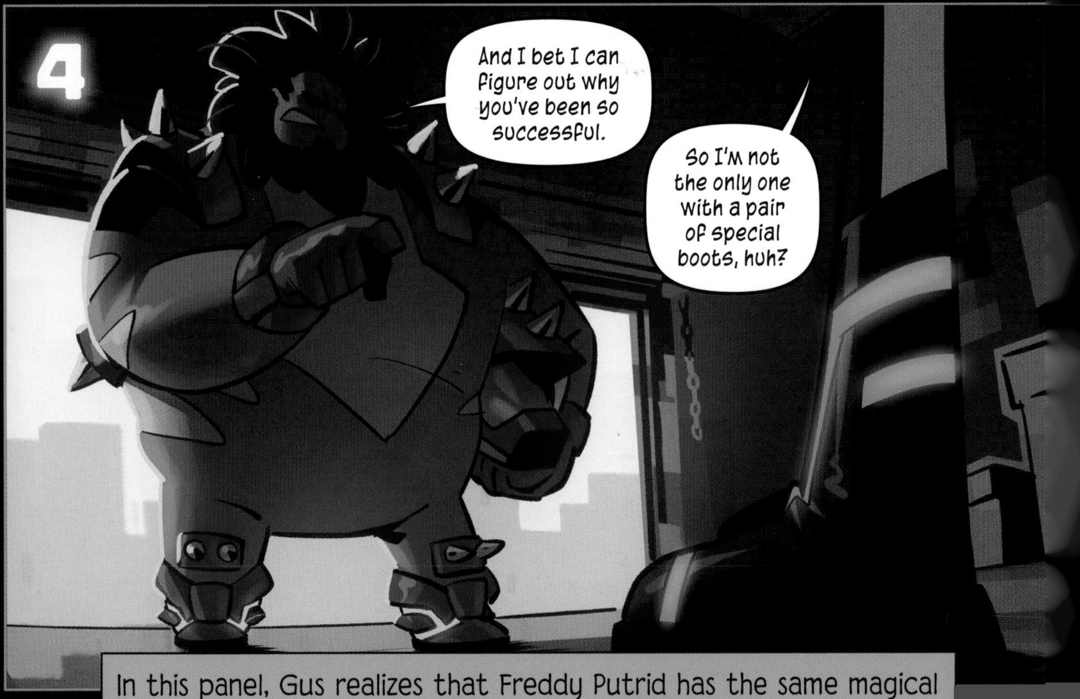
4
And I bet I can figure out why you've been so successful.
So I'm not the only one with a pair of special boots, huh?

In this panel, Gus realizes that Freddy Putrid has the same magical boots that he has. What clues in the art show this?

AUTHOR

Brandon M. Terrell (B.1978–D.2021) was a passionate reader, Star Wars enthusiast, amazing father, son, uncle, friend and devoted husband. He worked as an assistant director and producer on numerous independent films and commercial productions, as well as writing for the "Choo Choo Bob Show." Brandon received his undergraduate degree from the Minneapolis College of Art and Design and his Master of Fine Arts in Writing for Children and Young Adults from Hamline University. Brandon was a talented storyteller, authoring more than 100 books for children in his career. In Brandon's memory, consider picking up a Stephen King novel or a comic book, re-watching *The Mandalorian*, reading an old Hardy Boys adventure, and saving an open seat for the next Star Wars movie.

ILLUSTRATOR

Omar Lozano lives in Monterrey, Mexico. He has always been crazy for illustration and is constantly on the lookout for awesome things to draw. In his free time, he watches lots of movies, reads fantasy and sci-fi books, and draws! Omar has worked for Marvel Comics, DC Comics, IDW, Dark Horse Comics, Capstone, and several other publishing companies.

GLOSSARY

antique (an-TEEK)–something that is really, really old–even older than your grandparents

circuit (SUHR-kuht)–a series of races that leads to a single championship

contender (kuhn-TEN-dur)–a person–or shapeshifting cat–who has a good chance of winning something

emporium (em-POHR-ee-uhm)–a large store that sells a variety of items like auto supplies

last will and testament (LAST WILL AND TESS-tuh-muhnt)–a legal document that says what a person who has died has left to those still living, even including magical boots

mechanic (muh-KAN-ik)–a person who works on vehicles

retire (ri-TIRE)–to give up a line of work

souped-up (SOOPD-UHP)–having lots of cool improvements and accessories added

trio (TREE-oh)–three of something–such as three annoyingly cocky siblings

AWESOMELY EVER AFTER.

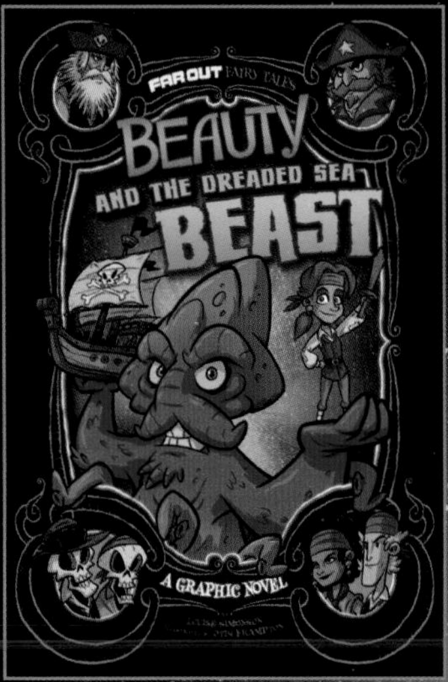
FAR OUT FAIRY TALES
BEAUTY AND THE DREADED SEA BEAST
A GRAPHIC NOVEL

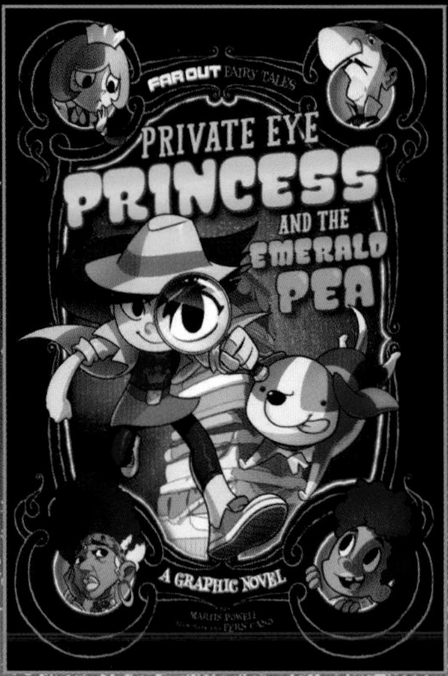
FAR OUT FAIRY TALES
PRIVATE EYE PRINCESS AND THE EMERALD PEA
A GRAPHIC NOVEL

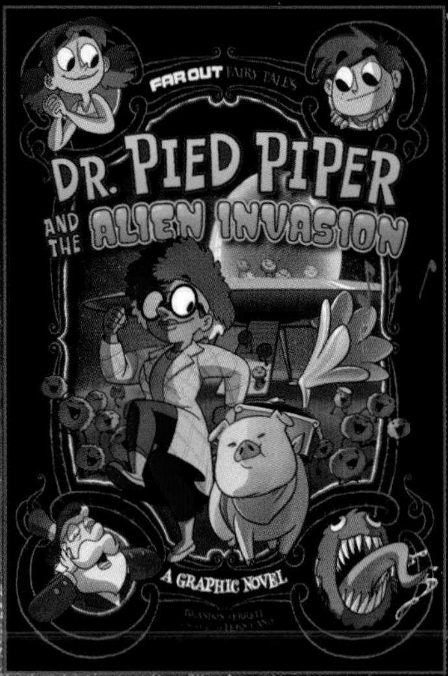
FAR OUT FAIRY TALES
DR. PIED PIPER AND THE ALIEN INVASION
A GRAPHIC NOVEL

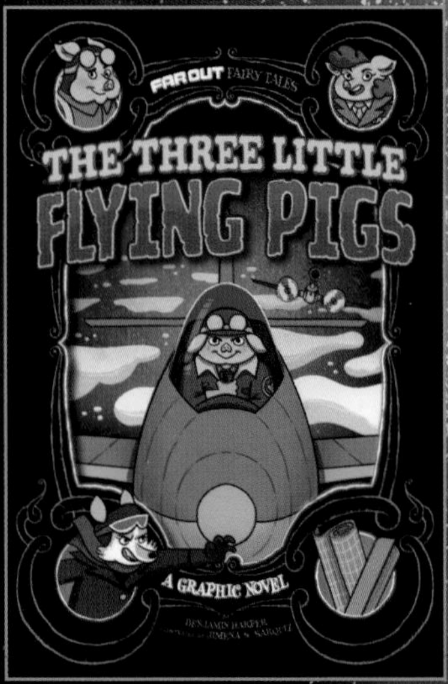
FAR OUT FAIRY TALES
THE THREE LITTLE FLYING PIGS
A GRAPHIC NOVEL

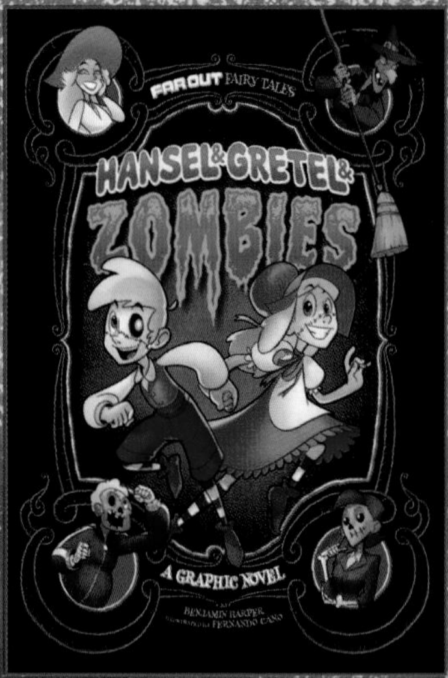
FAR OUT FAIRY TALES
HANSEL & GRETEL & ZOMBIES
A GRAPHIC NOVEL

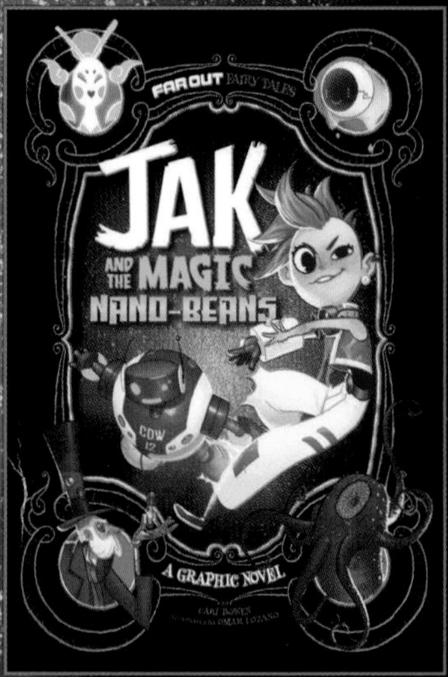
FAR OUT FAIRY TALES
JAK AND THE MAGIC NANO-BEANS
A GRAPHIC NOVEL

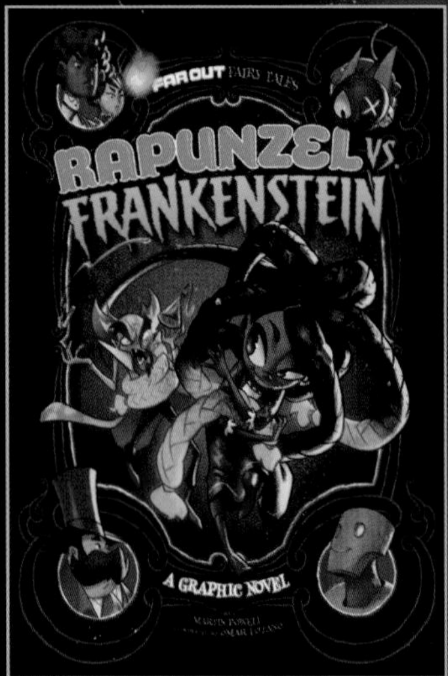
FAR OUT FAIRY TALES
RAPUNZEL VS. FRANKENSTEIN
A GRAPHIC NOVEL

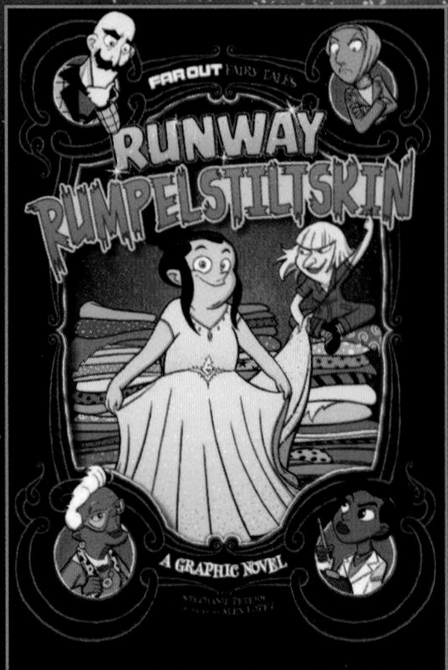
FAR OUT FAIRY TALES
RUNWAY RUMPELSTILTSKIN
A GRAPHIC NOVEL

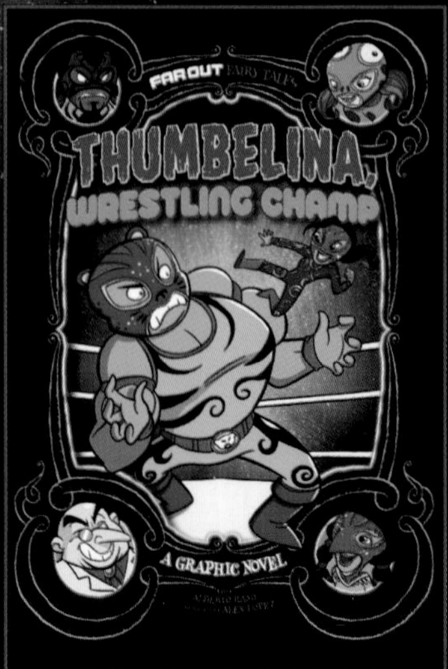
FAR OUT FAIRY TALES
THUMBELINA, WRESTLING CHAMP
A GRAPHIC NOVEL